The Fluff

Dedication: Of course to my sweetheart since 1986, Debbie.

Stephen Ambrose, "D-Day", "Up the Bluff at Vierville": "[Brig General Norman] Costa was accosted by a sailor whose LCT had been destroyed. Brandishing a rifle, he asked, 'How do you work one of these? This is just what I wanted to avoid by joining the Navy – fighting like a foot soldier."

That line became this story.

Anyone who writes about D-Day owes a debt to Cornelius Ryan and Stephen Ambrose, authors of the two greatest works about that event: "The Longest Day" and "D-Day."

Acknowledgements and Thanks:

Susan and Joe Vass, the first people outside my house to encourage me in the project.

The Internet, which provided me with many resources about D-Day, the USS Samuel Chase and the Coast Guard during WWII. The most helpful single item was an oral history with Marvin Perrett by Scott Price of the USCG Historian's Office, collected in 2003. Mr. Price also encouraged me to develop this story.

Mr. Perrett died in 2007.

Cover art: "Assault Wave" by Dwight Shepler (August 11, 1905 – September 2, 1974)
Courtesy of Navy Art Collection, Naval History and Heritage Command

Prologue

"Daddy, what are the things in this box?" Tip asked.

David brought the shadow box down from the top shelf. "This is from the war."

"Why is it up there? It's been too high for me to look at it."

"I put it up high so you'd be old enough to understand a little when you asked."

"Am I old enough?"

"Well, you're in second grade. And if you're old enough to ask, I'll try to answer," David said. "What do you know about the war?"

"A war is when a lot of people are fighting. My teacher said he was in Word War Two and it was very bad. A lot of people were killed. But what does that mean?"

"World War Two, princess. Let's see. Your teacher is Mr. Garcia. He was in infantry. That's probably the hardest job in a war. He's right that the war was very bad. He had friends killed. All my friends came through, but I knew men who were killed.

"We talked about being dead when Great Grandpa died. It's sad when people die when they are very old or maybe they are sick. They go to God but it's sad to lose the time they would have had on Earth and we're sad when we lose them.

"It's much sadder when people make each other die, when people kill each other, to take away the time someone was going to have.

"About twenty years ago, some very bad people were running Germany and Japan. Those countries are our friends now but they were taking over other countries and killing their people and we had to stop that. Many people died, lost their time on Earth because of the wicked people. We had to have a war to stop them.

"I got in the war in 1942, when I was eighteen. It was before God put Mommy and me in love, but Mommy knew me at school and at church.

"When I was in the war, I was in the United States Coast Guard. So that's the shield here at the top. A lot of people called us 'sailors' but we liked 'Coastie' better because we were a different branch." David paused and smiled. "We were proud of being different from the Navy even though we were sailing Navy ships.

"I was a bosun's mate, second class. That's the eagle here with the two stripes. I wore that on my sleeve on my uniform." He got a picture off of a lower shelf.

"You've seen this picture. See my hat where it says Coast Guard? And the patch on my sleeve."

"What are the round things with the pretty cloth parts?"

"Those are medals. You've seen cartoons where Bugs Bunny or somebody is wearing a lot of medals on his coat?"

Tip laughed. "Oh, yes."

"These are real medals. Men and women who served our country wear them to remember the brave things they did. The country gave them to us to tell us 'thank you' for doing those things. But we only wore them on our uniforms.

"This one is the Bronze Star. A lot of us got the Bronze Star, mostly for being where the shooting went on."

"This medal has stars on it."

"That's called a campaign medal. It's for serving in Europe. And this one is for serving in the Pacific Ocean. The stars are for the times we were fighting. This one is called the Victory Medal. We all got this when the war was over."

"What's the purple one with the heart on it? And who is on it?"

David smiled again. "It's called the Purple Heart. The man is George Washington. Put your hand here, princess," he said and held her hand to his scalp. "Can you feel that ridge?"

"Yes."

"That's called a scar. If my hair was very short, people could see that. If I go bald, everyone will see it! The Purple Heart is for people who got hurt by the enemy and that's where I got hurt. I thought it was silly because it was a small cut but the Coast Guard gave me the medal anyway."

"What's the rifle for?"

David paused and looked at it for a long moment. "I'll tell you the short version today. Someday I'll tell you the long version. I got this from an Army officer. He sent me a letter late in 1944 and this was with it. He'd been fighting through Europe and the letter took a couple of months to find me. The rifle is called the Combat Infantry Badge. Only infantry soldiers like Mr. Garcia wear it but the captain sent it to me because I had fought with him on D-Day."

Tip frowned at David. "I've heard about D-Day. That was when the war ended and the Germans lost."

"Well, not really. That was when the Allies went into France and started to push the Germans out. It was another year before the war was over in Germany.

"My main job was to run a landing boat – we called it a Papa boat. On D-Day, my boat blew up. When my boat blew up, I had to get onto the beach. I found some soldiers, or maybe they found me. I got my head cut when my boat blew up and one of the soldiers, a man named Tim, helped me wrap it up. I had to fight beside them all day. That's why their captain sent me the badge with the rifle."

Tip was pointing below the medals and the CIB. "That cross thing is broken."

David breathed deeply. "How do I tell my daughter this? And someday Andrew." "The cross goes with the rifle. That's an Iron Cross. It's a German medal for their brave soldiers. I broke the cross. I shot the man who was wearing it and he died. I killed another man that day and I shot two more men. I'm pretty sure one of those men was okay but I'll never know about the other one."

Tip gasped. "You killed him? Them?"

Andrea leaned on the kitchen door frame, watching them. David looked at her. "We knew we'd have to tell them about this someday," Andrea said.

"Yes, princess, I killed them. They were going to kill the men I was with. Maybe even kill me. So I had to stop them. That's why I got the Bronze Star and that's why the captain sent me the rifle badge.

"And that's why I kept the Iron Cross. I found the man who wore it later and I brought it with me so I'd always remember he was a man. Just like I was a man."

"But he was a bad man," Tip said.

"At least bad men had sent this man to do bad things," Andrea said. "One of those men killed your Uncle Walter, just when the war was almost over."

"Who was my Uncle Walter?" Tip asked.

Andrea took down another photo of three teenagers and sat on the couch. "You know your Uncle Steve is my older brother. Uncle Walter was older than both of us. Uncle Walter and Uncle Steve were soldiers. The Krauts killed Uncle Walter."

"Is that why we hate the Krauts?" Tip asked. "Like in the movies?"

David smiled sadly. "Andrea is awfully angry to this day because of Walter," he said to himself. "Princess, we hate what the Germans did. Sometimes that turns into hating the people who did it but I hope that will stop."

Tip had lost interest in the shadow box for the moment. She said, "I'm going to go read now," and skipped toward her room. David took Andrea's hands. "I pray for Walter every day," he said. "And for you."

Andrea smiled sadly back. "I know. I'm still mad at the Krauts."

David lifted the shadow box back to its place on the high shelf. "I was never mad at the Germans."

"To Write Myself Man"

June 5th, 1942.

"We're sending you into a world at war. Some of you are going to fight that war. Some of you are going to wait while the men you love fight it. Some of you are going to build what the fighters need. And some of you are going to lose your friends, your brothers, your sons.

"That is for tomorrow, a week from now, months from now. Today is graduation day, and we are proud of each of you. Your parents and families are proud of you. Please stand and prepare for the presentation of diplomas."

David stood. "This cap and gown seem a little silly. But high school is over. What's next?" He found his place alphabetically, about two-thirds of the way down the line of two hundred capped and gowned classmates. "Men and women. Well, maybe. Diana's been a woman all through high school and who knows what it would take to make a woman out of Christina? Me, a man? In the making, maybe. A lot will have to happen before I 'write myself man' as the old stories say."

The line progressed. "God be with you, Michael. God be with you, Sandra. God be with you, Maria. I know only a few of you, but every one of you is God's own." David discovered what many had learned before: at a moment like this, time flowed rapidly and it flowed slowly at the same time. The progression of names was tedious but he was glad for each classmate's moment to be singled out. "Lyle Granger. This is probably the first time someone's said something about Lyle and not mentioned his brother." David knew Lyle only slightly; Lyle's brother James was a school athletic legend from a few years earlier.

The line went on. The distance to the stage was down to about forty feet, David guessed. Then about ten. Then a girl he had once helped with a report was crossing and he was next. "David Ryerson," the announcer said, and David stepped out. "With honors."

Principal Morris and the mayor were conducting the ceremony. The principal handed David an empty diploma case – David knew they were empty; they'd been told to get their diplomas when they returned their caps and gowns, so that they would all get their own and avoid any mix-ups. The principal had the case in his left hand and placed it in David's left hand as they shook. David scarcely knew Principal Morris, having been studious and well-behaved but not much involved in activities. The mayor, a man David had never even seen before this evening, also congratulated him and shook his hand as if David were his own son. "This is quite an honor," David thought, "but he would have trouble recognizing me tomorrow if I bumped his car. I learned something in civics class and even more in the election in 1940."

The Presbyterian minister closed the ceremony with a benediction. Two hundred new "men and women" went to the tables where their diplomas were arranged by name groups. David took off the mortarboard cap and the knee-length gown. He was wearing his only suit, his only white shirt and his only tie. He draped the honor graduate stole around his neck. Then he detached his tassel and put it in his lapel's button hole. Mr. Thompson, his physics teacher, was at the table. "David, son, congratulations. Here's yours." He gave David the stiff certificate and checked the name. David put it into the diploma case.

His mother and father were moving through the chattery crowd; with two hundred graduates and their families and friends, the stadium probably held a thousand people or more. "Oh, darling, we're so proud!" his mother said as she hugged him. His father was shaking his hand and Daniel, his younger brother, was patting him on the back. Marianne, his little sister, got in to hug him around his waist.

Dinner was like a birthday party; David's grandparents had come for the occasion and they had cake and ice cream. The adults sat up talking until rather late and David was included as something nearly an equal. Floating over all the conversations was the topic around which everyone steered carefully: now that David was eighteen and had graduated, what was he going to do about the war?

David came down early the next morning and found Dad was waiting for him. Dad had a cup of coffee in front of him; for the first time in David's life, Dad poured a cup for him. "I draw the line at cigarettes," Dad laughed and David thought the laugh was nervous. "Dad's almost as scared of this conversation as I am. But we have to have it.

"Am I afraid? Maybe just awkward. Just awkward?"

Dad sipped and looked at David. David added some cream and sipped as well. "I'll have to start this. My whole family will be touched by this, but it's going to happen to me." "Dad, I'm going to enlist. You figured I would. All of the boys have been thinking about what to do."

Dad nodded. "You were boys. You're men now. You can bet that most of you are going to be drafted unless you enlist first. What service do you think you want to join?"

David had thought a lot about it. "You were in the Army but I think I'm going to try to go in the Coast Guard."

"Why do you think Coast Guard? You know the Coast Guard is going to pretty much join the Navy – already has, in fact."

David paused. "How do I tell Dad about this? It almost makes me sound like a coward." To his father, he said, "For one thing, there's a small chance of being stationed in the U.S. instead of overseas. But that's a small chance.

"Here's the important thing. I know we have to fight. But I don't want to kill anyone myself. Unless I'm a gunner of some kind, a Coast Guard job means being one step away from having to kill men. I don't know if I could kill someone."

Dad nodded. "You've been hunting since you were twelve but that's different."

"For one thing, squirrels don't shoot back. But I felt proud when I got my buck in October. I did care about him as an animal but I made a clean shot, we used the meat, and an animal isn't a man."

Dad took a long sip. "I was on the line for just a few months. I don't know if I ever killed a man. We were just shooting at the Germans. Just spray and pray. Men fell in front of us and that was all I knew. Then I got hit myself and that was the end of the war for me." Dad lifted his shirt. David had seen the scars on his father's belly a few times and he had known they were from "the war." But this was the first time Dad had described the battle itself.

David spoke again. "Everyone who goes to war could get killed or torn up. I know that. Everyone who goes to fight is part of the killing, too. But I'd rather be a step back if I can. Be a sonar man, or work on engines. Besides, when the war is over, maybe I'll know something that will help me work through college."

"That's good thinking, son. The Army's going to need a lot of riflemen but that's of little use when the war is over.

"You could be a medic, you know. The Army will need a lot of medics and so will the Navy. That might get you ready for medical school after the war. And you wouldn't have to carry a gun."

David smiled. "Maybe I'll try to be a medic. But I think I'd rather be an engineer or an architect than a doctor. And when the war's over, what is a medic going to do? There are only a few jobs for ambulance drivers and women have all the jobs at hospitals.

"The Army and the Marines have got some jobs like mechanics and drivers but the Coast Guard has more." David smiled. "Besides, you talked about the trenches a few times and how nasty they were. The ships take the beds and the kitchen with them everywhere."

Dad laughed. "Yes, but it's hard to sink a trench. You rarely hear much about the Coast Guard in time of war, mostly about their rescue work and smuggling work in peacetime." He grew serious. "You turned eighteen in March. I showed you in the newspaper that the draft board was going to start looking at this year's eighteen-year-old men right after graduation, so you may get a draft notice any day now."

"Is there any reason to wait for it?" David asked. "Besides the fact that I'd really rather keep working at the store and skip the whole war."

"Funny as it sounds, there is. The armed forces have been expanding for a year or two now but it's going a lot faster. One purpose of the draft is to space out how fast men are joining. But if you go to the recruiter yourself, you have the best chance of getting into the Coast Guard instead of just getting the next slot that the board has been told to fill. Most of those spots will be in the Army and the rest will be in the regular Navy."

"I saw an article in the newspaper that said volunteers had a better chance of getting jobs they want. What do you think of that?"

Dad smiled. "'The Army giveth and the Army taketh away.' It always did and I bet it always will. All the military services do. You may get a promise from the recruiter that is meant to be fair and honest, but the service you join is going to put you where they think they need you now. That part is just a roll of the dice." Dad sat quietly again. "I've run out of anything to say," David said to himself. Mom came about ten minutes later and the bustle of breakfast relieved the two men of the need to find something to say.

After breakfast, Dad took David to the garage for a minute. "I want you to take today for fun and rest," Dad said. "There's going to be little enough of that for a long time, son. And I'm going to call Pastor Dan and ask if he can speak with you before church tomorrow."

"I'll take Dan and Marianne fishing, maybe," David said. "May I use the car, please?"

"Sure, this afternoon," Dad said.

"David! Come in, son. Or is it time to stop calling you 'son'?"

David sat in the chair across the desk from the pastor. "This is my first time in your office," he said. "It always seemed like a mystery to me."

"Pastors are often mysteries to the children of their flocks," Pastor Dan smiled. "Even to the adults, too often. We're just men, though. I was a doughboy like your dad. A high-school graduate like you are now. You know my son; he's only twelve and I'm hoping the war will end before it pulls him in." He poured two cups of coffee and offered David the cream pitcher.

"Suddenly adults are offering me coffee but I still need a little cream," he said.

Pastor Dan shook his head a moment. "I know people who judge a man by how he takes his coffee. It's pretty foolish. That's just how you like your coffee. Manhood is a lot more than that.

"Your dad asked me to see you but he said you'd explain why. Your move, young Mr. Ryerson." He leaned back in his chair and put his hands together in his lap.

"You know the boys – the men – in my age group are going to come up for the draft very soon." Pastor Dan nodded. "I want to guard lives instead of taking them. Even Japanese or Germans."

"That's a proper sentiment, David. I'm sure there's more to this."

"What do I do if it comes up? If I find myself with a weapon and the enemy?"

Pastor Dan looked at David – intently, not threatening or judging, but intently. "If it really comes upon you, David, it's going to happen too fast to ask yourself any questions. You'll shoot or you'll get shot. That's what happened to me."

"You killed a man?"

Pastor Dan nodded. "All of the men in my company shot at the enemy but I'm one of only a few who had a close fight. I was twenty years old and I had worked as a mechanic before the war started. I heard the call to ministry a few years after the war.

"My squad was caught by surprise in the Argonne. I think the Germans were as surprised as we were, but instead of shooting almost blindly across a hundred or two hundred yards we were hand to hand, muzzle to muzzle.

"It was exhilarating even as it was terrifying. I pointed my rifle at a German's chest and I fired. My aim was high and I saw the bullet tear the German's head apart. He was dead before he fell. I checked to be sure and I saw he was barely a man – as I was barely a man. I've carried that ever since."

"You've felt guilty ever since? That would be almost twenty-five years."

Pastor Dan shook his head. "I did feel guilty for several years. It was at seminary that I put the guilt aside and realized I had done my duty. I was mistaken to think it was a sin. It was a terrible thing, but it was necessary.

"The German had his duty and his duty was more than to try to kill me. His duty, as he saw it, was to kill any American he could, as we were trying to kill any Germans we could. If I had paused and he had killed me, he probably would have killed other men from my squad. I was a corporal and I was responsible for those men. It would be too much to say that I thought about being responsible for them that minute, but I'd thought about it before the skirmish and I'm sure that's part of why I did what I had to do.

"The thing that really scared me after the fight was when I realized that I had found a terrible pleasure in it. The wildness of the melee, the power of destruction – I suddenly understood how some men could love this and I was terrified that I would love it. And in recognizing how I could love it, I came to hate it.

"I had the same experience with liquor but that story will be for another day."

"I'm hoping to get a job that won't involve shooting."

Pastor Dan looked keenly at David. "Every job in the military is part of the killing. Every job is dangerous in some measure."

"I think some people might think I'm a coward because I want to stay away from the killing. At least with my own hand. But I'd hate to have anyone think I'm a coward – especially my family."

"Your family knows better, David. They know how they raised you.

"I knew a lot of men who fought like tigers. Some of them were brave – they were confident in the face of danger. Some were courageous – they were afraid but they did what they had to do.

"I think most of the men were like you. They were afraid of battle but they were more afraid of being seen as cowards than they were of being wounded or being killed. And they fought as hard as any brave man or any courageous man.

"I was some of both – courageous but also afraid of being seen as a coward. I know I wasn't brave. If that fear of being a coward was a substitute for bravery or for courage, it served us well."

"I've always been pretty safe and pretty cautious," David said. "I know boys who raced their cars just to see what they could do and I always thought that was kind of foolish."

"There are going to be men who ride this war out in relative safety," Pastor Dan said. "You could be an aircraft mechanic, for example. The air bases will be targets but not like ships or infantry will be. And that work will be as necessary as gunners will be."

"And after the war, that work will be a good lead-in to a job," David said. "I've been thinking about that also. Dad plans to help me with college but then there's Dan and Marianne; I've got to be able to earn my way."

Pastor Dan nodded. "Being a mechanic or even a clerk won't make you a coward, David. Being a mechanic would be a pretty direct contribution to the war and we've got to win this war. This is a just war, I believe – the Japanese attacked us and the Germans have come to our coast to sink our ships."

David swallowed hard and finally said what he hated to say. "I am afraid, Pastor Dan. Whatever I do in this war, I might get killed or crippled. Dad spoke to me about his own wound for the first time yesterday. He's only rarely even let us see the scar."

"You're heading into a terrible thing, David. You should be afraid. Very afraid. God may guard you every inch of the way, but it's possible that God is going to give you strength to deal with terrible things. I know God will give you strength for terrible things, but I don't know if the terrible things will happen to you. You'll find out.

"It's almost time for service. Let's pray." The voices of the young man and the one-time soldier came together: "Our Father, Who art in Heaven..."

As they left the office, David grinned at Pastor Dan. "Maybe I should come back and you can tell me about liquor," he said. "Dad and Mom are teetotalers."

"As am I -- now. Maybe you should come back for that one."

"David, there are some ways we can make your boot camp easier," Dad said one evening. "Boot camp is a good place to blend in – a good place to listen as much as you can and to mostly keep your mouth shut. If we practice some drill and we practice locker discipline, you'll draw a lot less attention from the drill instructors – or whatever the Coast Guard calls their instructors. And believe me, you want as little of their attention as possible.

"The most important thing you can do is to follow instructions. When you're learning military skills and seamanship, that's pretty obvious. But it's just the same for drill, how you wear your uniform, how you take care of your locker and your bunk. The ones who listen best will get less trouble from the DIs and they'll spend their bile on the ones who pay less attention.

 "You've always been a tidy lad." A glance at Daniel, who had never been. "I'm going to set some special rules for your room until you leave for boot camp and I'll inspect your room every couple of days."

"I can do that, dear," Mom said. "Give me the rules and I'll check it every day."

"Will you yell as loud as I would if David gets things wrong?" Dad asked.

Mom laughed. "I've had very little practice yelling at David. I think I can learn."

"Very well, then, Sergeant Mom. But I'll work on the drill sessions."

That evening, after dishes, the family gathered in the kitchen. That floor was the hardest in the house and David stood in the middle. "I know you think you know how to stand up straight, David, but the military has a position called 'attention' that is a whole lot more 'stand up straight' than you're used to." Dad tilted David's chin down slightly. "Shoulders back and squared. Your thumbs right along the seam of your pants. Good. Heels together, feet at a forty-five degree angle." Marianne and Daniel giggled as Dad positioned David correctly.

"The command is 'attention' but it usually sounds like 'ten-hut.' If the sergeant tried to say 'attention' it would be hard to hear clearly. Same for a lot of the other drill commands – they are in forms that are easy to hear across a formation of men. Relax a minute, son.

"Any time you are in formation, you remain still and you speak only if you are spoken to. When you're at 'attention', you don't so much as look around or tilt your head.

"All right. 'Ten-HUT!'" David snapped into the posture his father had coached him into. "The command to relax is 'at ease.' Remember that it means to stay in place and remain silent, but you can relax your posture a little and you can move around a little, look around you if you want. You keep your right foot planted. 'At ease.'" David relaxed a little.

"From 'at ease', the only correct command is 'attention.' Sometimes men will give some other command from 'at ease' but that's the correct way. When the instructor or the sergeant is done with you, the command is 'dismiss' or it might be 'fall out.' The big difference is that 'dismiss' means they're really done with you but 'fall out' means to break up the formation and remain in the area.

"Ten-HUT!" David snapped back into position. "Very good. We'll practice a lot, even though you think you have it. It needs to become an instinct.

"Another common stance is 'parade rest.' Even though it's called 'rest', it's just a little less tight than 'attention' is. You snap your left foot out to twelve inches and you put your hands behind you." Dad demonstrated for David. "You can only go to 'parade rest' from 'attention' and from 'parade rest' you can only go to 'attention.' At least that's the right way to do it.

"You're at ease right now. Ten-HUT!" David came to full attention. "Parade HET." David snapped his left foot to position and put his hands behind his back. "Ten-HUT." David snapped his heels together. "Fall out. Which right now just means let me have the middle of the floor."

David moved over by the sink and Dad stood in the middle of the floor at attention. "Facing movements are done from the other foot – left face mostly by the right foot, right face by the left foot. About face is a right-foot action to your right. When you finish each facing movement, your heels will be together at attention. You can only do facing movements from 'attention.'" Dad went through the facing movements briefly. "It looks like you should finish the movements and still be just about where you started," David said.

"Your turn, son," Dad said. David took his place in the middle of the kitchen "Ten-HUT! At ease. Ten-HUT! Parade HET. At ease. Ah, caught you! Ten-HUT!." Marianne and Daniel giggled and Mom smiled.

"Will a drill instructor try to catch us like that?" David asked. "It seems like a cheap shot."

"Ours did and I thought it was a cheap shot too, but it does teach you to listen carefully. Especially when the whole squad gets an earful of rough language.

"Okay, you're at attention. Left FACE. Snap your heels together, son. Right FACE. About FACE." They spent about fifteen minutes practicing. "You're catching on very well."

The next morning, Mom and David went to his room together. Mom had a list in hand. "Here's what Dad has in mind for you."

"Socks at the left. Skivvies in the middle. Undershirts to the right. Shoes on a squared line under the bed. Picky, picky, picky, Dad."

Mom smiled. "Yes, but he knows about barracks life."

David nodded. "That, and I know on a ship I'm going to have just enough space to swing a cat. If it's a small cat and a short string."

"Here are all the rules for your closet, too. Let me give you an hour to get squared away."

"This will take a little practice but it's easy enough," David thought as he worked at rearranging according to Dad's exacting rules.

Mom came in an hour later. "Shoes nicely aligned," she said after checking with a ruler. "Drawers pass muster. But what's this, sailor?" She was trying to shout but she was laughing more than shouting. "That shirt has the left sleeve out instead of the right sleeve! Fix that right now!"

Through the summer, Dad drilled David most evenings and Mom inspected his room every day. Daniel began taking part in the evening drills; Marianne started "helping" Mom with the inspections. "Marianne, I already have two sergeants," David told her. "Two is enough, thanks very much."

That night, David prayed. "God, my family is a gift. Right down to this scruffy cat shedding on my blanket. Thank you, God, for all of them. Please keep them and me in the months to come. I'm hoping it will be shorter than years."

A few days later, Dad brought a book home after work. "David, it's taken me a few days to find this. I read it when I was about your age and it was a great adventure. But it also can teach you some things you'll need to know at sea."

"'Two Years Before the Mast.' Richard Dana. I've heard of it. Thank you, Dad!" David would read the book avidly over the next two weeks.

David and Dad had set the end of July as the time to move forward. "I've taken Monday off from work so we can go into Philadelphia," Dad said. "We'll get you signed up for the Coast Guard." David nodded. "Thanks, Dad," he said. "I know it'll put a hit on the gasoline ration."

Alone in bed, he prayed, "Dear God, the war is going to pull me in. I knew that. Please be with me through all of this. I have a long way to go, I have a lot of things to do, but I know You always will be with me." A few wide-eyed minutes later, he found himself thinking, "I call myself a faithful soul but somehow believing God is with me is doing very little for me."

Mom had breakfast ready early on Monday. Coffee – David was still getting used to coffee in the morning – and bacon, eggs and toast. The summer day was glorious as Dad started out of town and onto the highway to Philadelphia.

The city was reasonably familiar to David. "Independence Hall, the shipping in the river, crowds and crowds," he thought to himself. They found the recruiting station and a grizzled man in a dress uniform greeted them.

"Chief Bosun's Mate MacGregor," he introduced himself. "Retired about five years ago with twenty-four years' service. Got called back right after Pearl. Too old to go to sea, they told me, so here I am."

"Dad's hanging back. This is the first paragraph where I write myself man." "David Ryerson and this is my father, Michael," he said.

"All right, you think you want to join the Coast Guard. You know it's a lot like joining the Navy during a war."

"Yes, sir. There's also Beach Patrol and Harbor Security, though."

The chief nodded. "'Sir' is okay but 'chief' is better," he said. "'Sir' is for officers. Some people would think that asking for one of the stateside jobs is kind of soft." There was something of a challenge in the way the chief said this.

"Anyone with good sense would rather get a stateside job," David answered. "But those jobs are tougher than people think they are. They need doing too."

The chief nodded. "To be fair to you, son, you're a lot more likely to wind up as deckhand on a cutter than one of the horse boys on the beaches. Cutter duty is tough any time – they're light and fast, so they are rough when the seas or winds are high. We're putting a fair number of men into Navy ships, too – the Navy owns them but we're manning them. Mostly the transports and the landing craft and we're building a lot of those. The Coast Guard has been taking casualties already. Do you know much about small boats?"

"Dad and I have done some motorboating. That's about all I can claim. Some rowing."

"How well can you swim?"

David laughed. "That does seem like an obvious requirement. I can swim pretty well."

"Boy Scout badge? Swim team?"

"Just swimming in the lake where we go fishing. I taught my brother and sister how."

"Whatever the Coast Guard thinks you can do, we'll teach you how. Some of it you may learn the way a cat learns how to swim."

"Beg pardon, chief?"

The grizzled chief smiled and held his hand at arm's length as if he were holding a cat, then let go. "Splash!" David laughed.

"Here's where we start," the chief said and handed David a stack of forms to fill out. "Then we'll have the doctor look you over."

"How long are we likely to be yet?" David asked.

"In a hurry?"

"No, but Dad must be bored stiff." The chief glanced at where Dad was sitting with a Collier's magazine.

"Probably about an hour yet," the chief said.

"Dad, maybe you can go to a coffee shop or something and be back here in an hour." Dad nodded. "That sounds like a good idea," he answered and left.

David filled out line after line. "Press hard; it looks like there are four carbons. Date of birth: March 14, 1924. Place of birth: Pittsburgh, Pennsylvania. U.S. Citizen: yes. By birth." Then he filled out the medical history. "Hernia, no. Allergies, no. Heart disease, no. Major injuries, no. Measles, yes. Homosexual, no." It seemed an odd question.

The chief looked at the finished papers.

"Everything on the form is okay," the chief said. "Time for your physical." The chief led David to a room marked "Physical Examination." "Doc, here's our first for today," he said to a woman in a lab coat.

David paused. "I've never met a woman doctor," he said. She was relatively young as well – probably only about thirty and pretty.

"That's okay, young man, I've met a lot of men patients," she smiled. She was still checking David's medical history when the chief brought in another young fellow. "This recruit did his paperwork yesterday but you had left. Would you fit him in also, please?"

"Certainly, chief," she said. The doctor reviewed the other set of forms. "Both of you undress to your undershorts, please," she said.

"She asked so nicely. Probably the last 'please' I'm going to hear for a couple of years. It's fine taking my clothes off in front of this fellow but it sure feels funny taking them off for a woman. Almost like a sin."

She was used to this, apparently. "Come on, lads," she said. "Clothes on the hooks here." David and the stranger glanced at each other and they did as they were told. A few moments later they were standing in just their boxer shorts.

The doctor started by simply walking around both of them for a general inspection. "Mr. Land, the scar on your arm – from when you broke it?"

"Yes, ma'am," he answered. The doctor checked their vision with an eye chart. "Do you know the joke about the eye doctor in Poland?" she asked.

"Tell us," David answered.

"He asked the man, 'Can you read line 7?' And the man answered, 'I used to go out with her!'" The recruits laughed.

She examined their throats and ears, listened to their chests. She had them bend to touch their toes and stand on one foot with eyes closed to check their balance.

David gulped when he realized what had to be next. "Please lower your shorts, men," she said. "About mid-thigh."

"This is the first time a woman will see my...my penis. Well, there are harder things than this coming up." He pushed his shorts down as directed; so did the other recruit.

The doctor gently handled David's penis and put a gloved finger into his groin. "Turn your head and cough for me," she said. "Cough again, please. No, no sign of hernia. That's fine; you can put your clothes on." David's embarrassment had spared him a much worse embarrassment; he had felt the first stirrings of erection when the doctor had touched him.

"Well, men, for better or worse you're both in fine shape." She signed their medical forms. They had dressed as quickly as they could. David missed her glance of sympathy as they left the medical office. "Who knows what's ahead for them? A lot of work at the least. Cramped quarters and storms. And maybe a lot worse."

The chief was grinning a bit when they came out. "He's enjoying our embarrassment," David thought but he managed a smile himself.

"All right, you're both accepted. How soon can you leave?"

The man named Land answered first. "I've got my things at the hotel where you put me up. I can go tomorrow."

"Then tomorrow it is. How about you, Ryerson?"

"I didn't bring anything," David said.

The chief looked at a calendar and a list, made a mark. "Let's have you back on Monday, then," he said. "You're only going to need shaving gear and a change of clothes. You'll be sending your clothes home right after you get to boot camp anyway. Be here early; your train will leave about ten o'clock."

"How about books?" David asked.

"A Bible if you want, maybe one other book if it's small. There are going to be a lot of people offering you Bibles in the next few weeks. Matter of fact, the Gideons bring me boxes of them if you need one." The chief showed David a couple of boxes. "Here's one a lot of the lads have been taking. Pocket edition of the New Testament with Psalms and Proverbs. King James Version. If you need to travel light, that's a good choice. Print's too small for my eyes these days."

"What's that box?" David asked, picking up a small book. "That's an odd print."

"Hebrew," the chief said. "We get a few sons of Abraham and a couple of the rabbis bring me Hebrew copies of the Old Testament. English, too. The women at St. Pat's bring me Douay Bibles for the Catholics."

The chief knocked on a door. A youngish man came out; his uniform had gold stripes and a shield at each cuff. "Lieutenant, will you do the honors?"

David asked, "What honors?"

"Have to swear you in."

"Could we wait a minute, please? My dad would want to see this." By good luck, Dad was just coming into the office.

The officer shook hands with Dad. Then he said, "Men, raise your right hands and repeat after me. For God's sake, when I say 'state your name', though, use your name. It was funny the first twenty times but it's gotten old."

"I, David Mark Ryerson, do solemnly swear to bear true allegiance to the United States of America, and to serve them honestly and faithfully, against all their enemies or opposers whatsoever, and to observe and obey the orders of the President of the United States of America, and the orders of the officers appointed over me."

"You are now members of the United States Coast Guard," the officer said. He shook hands with the new "Coasties" and David's father; so did the chief.

"Congratulations, young man," Dad said and shook the other recruit's hand.

"I look just like I did when we drove here, but I'm different. I'm committed now. Legally bound." Dad was chatting about the scenery and the beautiful day, about Mom having dinner ready. "About anything except that I'm leaving."

"A few weeks ago I came to your office for the first time. Here I am again," David said. "Dad said I should talk to you about something – something he said you know more about than he does."

"Liquor," Pastor Dan said and smiled. "Your dad tells me he's never touched liquor, not even when he was in the Army. I'm sure it's true. Our church is a temperance church, though we're less strict among Methodists than among Baptists or some others."

"That's right. Dad always said it was foolish to put a thief in your mouth to steal your wits."

"Your dad asked me to talk with you because I've been in the bottle. What do you think you know about drinking?"

David smiled. "Not a darn thing. I've heard boys at school brag about drinking on the weekends but that's all. I've read about it in books. But I don't know that I've ever seen anyone who'd been drinking or was drunk."

"You will in the Coast Guard, sure as can be.

"Let me do a little set-up. I know your family well, son. Your dad and I have worked on projects here at church and talked a lot. Just as friends do. He's proud of you – all three of you. He's wanted to raise you in the best way he could. Most importantly to your dad, he wanted you to understand that his rules were for your well-being, not to hem you in or make you miserable. Your mom thinks the same way.

"I think it's worked. You haven't ever been defiant just to be a jerk or to see what you could get away with. You understand responsibility in a way that a lot of young men don't. You're cooperative rather than just obedient. Some boys get raised strictly but they only think it's to push them around instead of to get them ready to live well. Young men who see their parents living narrow lives and they think it's a prison.

"And some young men get raised like wolves. They have no rules or they have no rules that last and that's worse than no rules.

"But many responsible, intelligent young men – boys becoming men – get away from their parents and try some experiments with women or liquor. They have to work out some new rules and they try some things they've been told they're too young for. It's about curiosity and independence and it can sure get them into trouble."

"Dad and I have had some of that talk," David said.

"Of course you have. I'm the friend your father asked to help, not the father you don't have. But that's where the bottle comes in.

"I grew up with a father who drank sometimes. It was an ordinary family and an ordinary home; Dad was always sober but I'd see him with a beer or another drink.

"When I was at Army training in Texas, we were bored a lot of the time. You put a lot of bored young men in one big room and they'll do almost anything to break up the monotony. Throw in some who just like to break rules and some who are trying to tell themselves they are men now and there will be some trouble.

"The boys used to get into fights and wrestling matches a lot and I won a couple of them, lost a couple of them. We broke a couple of bunks and a couple of windows and wound up paying for them out of payrolls that were awfully small to start with.

"Then we went to France and it was even wilder. When we were in the trenches, we'd go a week without decent food or being clean and of course some shooting back and forth. If we'd been fighting more seriously, we'd have been less trouble to our sergeants, maybe. When we got to the rear for a few days, we'd be trying to forget the week and we'd really want to have some fun.

"So there was a lot of drinking. A lot of fights, a lot of whoring, a lot of venereal disease." Pastor Dan smiled a moment. "I stayed out of the whoring, at least. But I did some of the drinking and some of the fighting."

Pastor Dan looked somber. "Bad habits are hard to change. A lot of us thought, 'well, we'll get home after the war and we'll just go back to having a beer.' A lot of us found out we wanted a lot more than one beer when we got home. Partly habit, partly to forget what we'd been doing. Did I say forget? You still remember even when you're drunk. But you can pretend for a few hours."

He sighed deeply. "And then one day I woke up on the floor beside my bed in my parents' house. I had been drunk for two days straight but I realized I had been useless for a year, since I'd come home from France and been discharged. My parents had sheltered me and I had just been a drain on them."

"That would have been during Prohibition," David said.

"The Volstead Act took effect in January of 1920 but Prohibition only slowed drinking down a little. It was summer of 1920 that I cleaned up.

"Anyway, I did clean myself up and found a job at a garage the next day. I saved up some money and took a room of my own, saved more and worked harder and started praying again. I found myself in seminary, then ordained, then married and a father.

"I was a binge drinker rather than a full-blown drunk, so I could find my way back with prayer and some shouting from my parents. It was still awfully hard. For six months, I wanted to drink even though I was disgusted with the me that had spent those two years in the bottle. It would have been easier if I'd skipped the drinking. I'd recommend you skip it too."

David smiled. "And the whoring?"

Pastor Dan snorted. "Well, that goes without saying. More seriously, you're going to be lonely and bored a lot of the time. A night with a woman was just the medicine some men thought they needed.

"Well, some of them needed more medicine after that night. Some kept it up and got dosed three or four times. But even the ones that dodged venereal diseases, some of them realized that what they'd been doing was more insult than pleasure."

David swallowed hard. "I think that's all I want to know about that!"

"You're a young man and healthy. Of course you want to know more about the flesh. But whoring in a foreign land is a bad school. Really, I guess whoring anywhere would be a bad school."

"I've been too shy to date in high school. Well, at least I'll go to war without a girl being scared about me."

Pastor Dan smiled. "There are your mother and Marianne. And you may have missed it, but there are probably a few other girls."

"Two sons of our church are leaving this week to serve our nation in the dreadful war that is upon us. These are the first of our family of faith but there will be more. We will ask a special blessing for all of them in their turns. David Ryerson and Timothy Madison, come forward."

David knelt beside Tim at the altar. Pastor Dan put a hand on each of their heads. Their parents stood behind them and put hands on their shoulders. "Everyone, come forward, please. Those of you toward the back, put your hand on someone's shoulder or hold hands. Everyone, join the chain. Let the chain be a solid as our love for these young men. Let us all be as their mothers and fathers, their sisters and brothers. Yes, even the smallest – bring the youngest children to the front to touch these men, our brothers and sons. They are leaving us to guard these children."

David smiled at the little boy who was holding his left hand. "Conrad, I'm glad you're here. Do you still have that stained-glass window we made with tissue paper in Sunday School?"

"Yes, Mr. David."

"You're the firs to call me 'mister.' And I think you'll be the last for a couple of years."

By now nearly a hundred people were now crowded into the space between the front pews and the altar. When Pastor Dan was sure that everyone was in contact, he continued.

"In the Middle Ages, the ceremony that made a knight was a ceremony of faith and prayer. The knight was commissioned to use might for right, to defend the weak against the oppressor. So let it be now. We give our accolade to these young men. We commission these men, our sons. God the Father, Jesus the Savior, Holy Ghost, be with them through all that is to come. Strengthen their limbs as they need them. Strengthen their hearts even more than their limbs. Give them fortitude for hardship, courage for danger, skill for their tasks. Give them forbearance with the enemy when they can show forbearance. Give them the heart to do what they must, even if it must be terrible to them, and give them judgment to know how to do Your will in this terrible time. Give them hope, dear Jesus. Hope that they will come home and hope that, if they do not come home to their families, they will go home with You. Amen."

A chorus of "amen" rippled through the congregation. "Let us all go, then, to serve God's will," said Pastor Dan and the group broke up – reluctantly, it seemed to David.

It was an awkward day at David's house. "Let me help you pack," Marianne insisted.

"I only get one bag, you know. And a small bag at that."

"Well, you only shave a couple of times a week, and you already shaved today. So I can pack your razor and stuff." She carefully put the razor kit and the tube of shaving cream in his bag.

"Hey, leave my toothbrush. I still need that tonight," he said as she was busily sweeping his other things into the bag.

"Okay. Be sure you pack it in the morning. You'll need some underwear," she said.

"Those are my drawers in my drawers," David laughed. "Hey, just three sets, okay? Danny may need the others when he's a little bigger."

"Me? Why would I want your leftover underwear?" Daniel was watching Marianne with the same amusement as David.

Dad was leaning against the doorway. "If we have the kinds of shortages we did last time, you'll be glad to have that underwear," he said. "You know we already can't get tires. Only a little gasoline. Who knows what will be next? You'd better believe skivvies could run short. You could wind up wearing the shoes David sends home."

Marianne picked out a pair of pants and a shirt. "Do you need a sweater?" she asked.

"It's August. The Coast Guard is going to give me all kinds of weather gear before it gets cold, little one."

"Then you should be set," Marianne said. "Remember your toothbrush in the morning. What about your hair brush?"

Dad laughed. "Comb, maybe. David's hair is going to be too short to brush for a long time, Marianne."

Mom had prepared a favorite dinner: pot roast, corn on the cob, a chocolate cake. "This could be your last really nice dinner until you get home on leave," she said. "Take a little more."

David smiled. "The Coast Guard plans to feed me," he said. "Though of course you feed me a lot better."

"Will you get home on leave before you go to your first assignment?" Mom asked.

"We'll have to see. I think so," David answered.

They spent the evening listening to the dramas on the radio and chatting in stilted tones. David went to bed early. "God, be with us all. It's a long path, I'm sure it will be a weary path, and I can only see a little of it now. It turns out of sight. Will I choose the turns? Have You already chosen them? Will I serve honestly and faithfully?

"Will I come home?

"In everything, God, Thy will be done."

Boot Camp

Mom came with Dad on Monday to send David off. They arrived at the recruiter's office at nine in the morning. "Say your good-byes, son, I've got to get you to the train station," the chief said. "God be with you, son," Mom said. "God is with you, son," Dad said. "God be with all of you," David answered. His parents got back in Dad's car. David picked up his valise and put it in the official car as the chief pointed. He climbed in and the chief got behind the wheel.

"You know, son, you'll never go home. The man who goes home to your parents will remember the boy who just said good-bye, but he'll be someone different. He is supposed to be someone different. Even just from basic training and advanced training, you'll be more man than boy."

"Write myself man," David replied. "Time to write myself 'man.'"

"You're going to have to, son. All you boys will." The chief was parking at the train station now. "Got all your things? Ready for camp?"

"No, chief, but I bet no one ever is. I'm as ready as I can be, though."

"If you know you're not ready, you're already more ready than most of the boys I send. Good luck, son." The chief shook his hand and David boarded the train.

The train ride was only a couple of hours. David got off and looked around the platform. There were several other men grouped near a man in uniform. "Looking for Manhattan Beach, son?" he asked.

"Yes, sir."

"Name?"

"David Ryerson."

"From here on, recruit, you'll give your name as Ryerson, David. All the lists are by last name, of course. Line up with these men. There are just a few more coming."

David took his place quietly. "Here's a motley crew. Short, tall, that fellow must only be about seventeen. That one must be nearly thirty. I imagine we're all from the area."

One of the waiting men shook a package of cigarettes, drew one and lit it. "Smoke, friend?" he offered to David.

"That's quite a gesture. Smokes are going to be hard to get. How do I get out gracefully?" David asked himself. Aloud, he said, "Thank you, but I haven't tried smoking yet."

"Good for the nerves sometimes. I got started as a night watchman, bored to death." The man put the cigarettes away.

An hour later, three more men had joined them. "Let's go, men," said the petty officer. They went to a truck in the parking lot and climbed into the back. Rough wooden benches served as seats. The ten young men settled down and the truck ground away.

David watched the view out of the open back of the truck. "Leaving the city. Suburbs. The ocean. We're up to the camp gates. We're stopped."

"All out, boots," a gruff voice shouted. The first man was trying to figure out how to get out with his gear. "Hand it to me," David said. The man hopped down and David passed him his bags. It turned into a relay. The last man handed David his bags before he hopped down. "Fall in!" the petty officer ordered.

David immediately went in front of the petty officer and stood at attention. The other men milled around a moment before a second petty officer yelled at them. "Get in line with this boot! You, go to the left. You, left of him."

Another truck pulled up and a group of men scrambled out with their bags. "You men! Fall in behind these men." The two lines stood rather raggedly.

"Damnation, sometimes I think it'd be easier to make coasties out of women than the boys they keep sending me," the first petty officer said. "Huh?" one man said.

"You're in ranks, boot! Nobody asked you anything. When I want to hear from you, you'll know about it.

"All of you! Stand up straight. Get your heels together. You, pull your chin in. All of you, square those shoulders. You got nothing to be proud of yet, but you stand like you're proud. Hear me?"

Dave stood silently as the other men found places. The two petty officers moved among them, getting the men into some semblance of attention and being quite abrupt about it. The day was warm even with the breeze from the Atlantic.

"Now hear this. When you're in ranks or any formation, you will speak only when spoken. When you do speak to any of the training staff, your first word and your last word will be 'sir.' For you guys who think you're funny, if it's a woman, yes, say 'ma'am.' First and last. But you're gonna see precious few women.

"All right, you still have to learn 'right face' yet but everyone turn to your right. When I say 'forward, march', step off with your left foot and march through the gate. Whenever you're in a formation, you will always step off with your left foot. We'll get to real marching a little later."

"This is a factory," David thought. "We're raw material and here's where the manufacturing starts."

They were herded into a cavernous room with benches. "First thing you need is a seabag. Your whole life is going to fit into one of these." Each man received a large duffel bag with a drawstring closure. "You can use a padlock here," one of the petty officers showed them. "Set your bags in front of these benches."

"Come over here and get skivvies," one of the uniformed men said. There were a couple of men ready to issue the underwear. Each sized up the man in front of him and handed him several packages – shorts, undershirts, socks. "Come over here and draw dungarees." David went to the next counter; again, a quick glance to estimate his size and three pairs of denim pants and three cambric shirts came his way. "Next table for shoes," the sailor told him.

David told the next sailor, "Sir, size 11, please, sir." "Going by the look on your face, we're the only people who ever call you 'sir'", David thought.

The sailor rummaged and handed him two pair of shoes and a pair of puttees. "Hope they'll do," the sailor said and got shoes for the next man. The next table had hats. The last item of issue was a hardbound book with a blue cover. "The Blue Jacket's Manual", David read. "US Navy?"

David carried his pile of clothes to his place. "All right, every man jack of you, get your clothes off and put them in your luggage." David looked around. "Like a locker room. We've all done this before." He sat and got his clothes off; others overcame their reluctance and followed suit. They dressed, folded their new clothes and got them into the seabags. "Well, the shoes will do, I guess," he thought. "The puttees are kind of funny." He got them buttoned on, doing his best to look like the Coast Guardsmen around them. "This is almost like putting our old selves away. Our old selves from this morning," he thought as he and the other men packed their civilian clothes away.

"Fill out these tags and put them on your suitcases. We'll get them home for you," said a man at the exit. "Remember, you wear your cover at all times when you're outdoors. At all times."

"Well, we kind of look like sailors," David said to one of the strangers near him.

"We call ourselves 'coasties. And you'll look more like coasties after the next stop," one of their shepherds said. They formed up outside with their seabags. A short, ragged march took them to their next stop. "I have no idea where we are on the post," David thought.

 "All right, left line first, in here."

"The barber shop," David thought. "More like a Wyoming sheep-shearing," he thought a moment later. "Those first two men took about a minute each. Yes, supplies, that's what we are. Raw material, anyway." Then it was his turn. He sat in the chair and the barber whisked the cloth over him. "Ouch! Dang clippers are hot!" he thought. The hot clippers ran roughly over his head; he tried to hold still and the barber used one hand to brace his head. The cloth whisked off. "Next!" the barber called. David felt the stubble on his scalp as he went out. "Get your cover on!" he heard and quickly put the hat on his head.

Their company formed up with their seabags. "Fall in! Headed for the barracks next," their shepherd said. "Seabags over your left shoulders. Right HAPE." David executed the turn as smartly as he could with a fifty-pound bag on his shoulder. "A couple of the men have had some coaching," he thought as he looked around without turning his head. "The others are just turning to their right."

"Ford, HART." They stepped off, most of them on their left feet. The group half-marched, half-shuffled for a few hundred yards. "Halt!"

"And two," David thought to himself. The man ahead of him had stopped instantly and the one behind took two steps instead of one. "Kind of squashed," he thought.

"Get your intervals again," their shepherd ordered. "Left HAPE." They were in some kind of formation at least. "When I say 'dismissed', take one step backward with your left foot and say 'ay, aye, sir.' Always start with your left foot. Break ranks and go into the building in front of us. As you go down the aisle between the racks, take the first open rack. Start to the left. Put your seabag in front of your foot locker and stand by the rack. We'll talk about stowage in a minute.

"Dis-MISSED!"

David and the others took a step backward. "Aye, aye, sir," came in a ragged chant. They broke up the formation and went into the barracks. David found himself paired with a man about his own age at the third double rack on the left.

"I'm David Ryerson," he said, smiling and extending his hand. The smaller man took it.

"Giovanni Zirilli. From Little Italy, but you was gonna figure that out."

"Shall I take the top, then?"

"What, 'cause I'm five-four and you're about six feet?"

"Well, yes."

Giovanni smiled more broadly. "I hoped you'd say that, really. I could get up there but it'll be a lot easier for you."

"Everyone to the center. Let's get your names and your racks figured out."

"Sir, Zirilli, Giovanni. Bottom rack. Sir"

"Sir. Ryerson, David. Top, sir."

"Mutt and Jeff act. Got a lot of those." The petty officer continued down the aisle.

"Everyone to center here. All right, I'm your company commander. Machinist's Mate Second Class Fulton. You ain't gonna use my name to my face and you're likely gonna call me things I don't wanna hear behind me. I can live with that but you'll be sorry if I do hear you.

"The most important phrase for you to learn just now is 'aye, aye, sir.' You use it in response to an order and it means you are going to carry it out. 'Yes, sir,' is for any other reason you need to say yes.

"We call a bed a 'rack.' I got no idea how you recruits maybe made your racks at home. In my bay, you're gonna make your rack the Coast Guard way. It may seem stupid to you and, y'know, I don't care if it does. But I'll explain it because everybody these days seems to think he gets an explanation.

"First, you're gonna learn a lot of jobs that have to be done fast and done right. If you bog down just making your rack, God only knows what kinda stupid stuff you're gonna do when you have to lower a boat in a storm 'cuz one o'you foul-ups fell off the ship and the OOD decides it's worth trying to get your sorry ass back.

"Second, if this place looks like a pig-stye, you're gonna think like pigs. That's okay if you just wanna wind up bacon some day but it ain't no way to win a war. Even more in the berthing area at sea, crowded like it will be."

"More crowded than this bay?" Giovanni asked.

"Don't remember askin' you to say nothin', recruit. And remember to start and finish with 'sir.' Son, when you get to your ships, this place will seem like a hotel.

Four 'r five deep, two men in three racks, just enough room to swing a dead cat. If it's a small cat."

David smiled to himself. "Why do we always talk about swinging dead cats? Keep that grin off your face, David, or you'll draw his eye and this is a bad time to stand out."

By odd luck, though, he had caught the petty officer's eye after all. "You, there. Name."

"Sir, Ryerson, David. Sir."

"Well, then, recruit Ryerson. Do you think you know how to make a rack?"

"Sir, I'll do my best, sir. Please tell me how you want it done, sir."

The petty officer grinned wryly. "That was a pretty good answer, son. You get started right here with your own rack. I'll let you know if you're off. But do it slow for the others to see."

David found a set of linen on the rack. He laid the items out on the footlocker. Opening the first sheet, he spread it widely. At the head, he carefully folded the sheet under the mattress – "kinda thin, that," he thought – and smoothed it under the mattress on the springs below. "Get the bottom edge just to the mattress foot, all the slack at the head," he thought. He carefully and slowly pulled the slack of the sheet onto the mattress to make a triangle on top of the mattress Then he smoothed the lower part under the mattress.

"Hold up a minute, recruit. See how some of the sheet is poking through? Smooth that out. You only get a little slack on that when we inspect." David passed his hand under the sheet and smoothed it. "Why is he so particular?" he asked himself.

And heard. "Lotta your work will be out of sight after you do it. But it's gotta be done right or maybe somebody gets killed. I ain't kiddin'. I seen it."

David went to the other side and pulled the sheet taut. At the corner, he made a point of carefully looking under the mattress and smoothing the sheet.

He laid out the top sheet and Fulton stopped him. "Go ahead and spread one blanket, recruit. Then you can make them as one job. Faster and you're going to have plenty to do after you make your rack." David proceeded to arrange the sheet and blanket. He put his only pillow into its case and laid it on the rack. "Sir, I don't know how you want me to use the second blanket, sir."

"Fold the second blanket in half. Now lay it over the pillow to this point. Everybody look at where he's got the lower edge of the blanket. When I look down the bay, I want all the pillow covers in line. You'll find out if I think they're a-kilter."

David laid the folded blanket over the pillow. "T'other way, recruit. Put the fold toward the foot. That's it. Now make hospital corners here at the head."

David silently arranged the blanket and looked under the mattress. He smoothed out some tufts of the blanket that covered the pillow.

"That ain't perfect but it was a good start, son. I'm guessin' you was coached. Or did you work in a hospital?"

"Sir, my father was in the Army in 1918. He coached me, sir." Fulton abruptly pulled the linens off the bed. "All right, then, all of you get your racks ready."

"There's just space enough between the racks to work," David thought as he remade his rack. Giovanni was working opposite him.

"Hey, we can help each other. Let's just work each side," Giovanni said. That worked out well. David saw that Fulton had spotted their cooperation but he didn't say anything to stop them.

"Fall in by your racks at attention," Fulton called. He went down the lines, pointing out where he thought the work was sloppy. "That was the easiest inspection you're gonna get, recruits. After this, I'll be very particular. Nasty, some of you are gonna say."

They formed up next at one of the lockers for an extensive lesson on putting their gear away. "You think is just to make your life tough, but when you're trying to dress in the dark and the ship is heelin' and wheelin', you'll think kinder of me."

Over the next hour, they got their personal equipment square. That was followed by their introduction to drill.

"Ryerson, come to the middle here." David went and stood in front of Fulton. "I was watchin' and your dad, I bet it was, taught you some drill, too. Or Boy Scouts?"

"Sir, my father coached me, sir."

"Then you'll do for a demonstration. Ten HUT." David snapped to attention. "See how he stands tall. Chin level, shoulders back. Feet about 45 degrees. Thumbs on his seams. Now, all of you – ten HUT."

David kept in place as Fulton went up and down the line. "Shoulders back, Milton. Chin square, you lunk – you got it stuck out like you got a glass jaw. Heels, recruit. Heels together."

They did Parade Rest and Fulton again went up and down the line. "Your left hand is inside and your right hand is out," he said to several recruits. "Gawd, I hope you know your right and your left, at least."

He came back to David. "Now, the facing movements is a little tricky. When you face, you go on the heel of the foot where you're goin' and you push with ball of t'other foot. Ryerson, do it kinda slow. Left HAPE." David demonstrated. "See how his hands stay put on his seams.. When you're really good, only your feet and legs move. You could do it with a book on your head. Right HAPE." David returned to his starting position. Fulton put the group through alternations of Left Face and Right Face, always moving up and down, always finding fault.

"All right, Ryerson, I got a real test for you. About HAPE."

"Yep, I thought that was coming," he said to himself. He put his right foot back and pivoted, right ball and left heel, and he finished with his heels together. "Son, your dad did a good job. You should tell him that when you write home."

"Sir, I will, sir."

"Salutin'. Our covers ain't got brims so you salute to your eyebrow. Same if for some reason you're salutin' but you don't have your cover on, but you only do that in an office. Your hand comes up your center line and down the same way. The command is 'hand SALUTE.' If I want you to hold the salute, the command will be 'Present ARMS.' Y'hold 'Present Arms' until you get the command 'Order Arms.'"

"Present. HART." All of the men presented salutes. "Some are snappier than others," David thought to himself." Fulton clearly thought so also; again he made rounds in the company and corrected men he thought were less sharp.

When they had done stationary drill for about fifteen minutes, Fulton said, "Now you gotta learn how to march. You only learn to march by marchin' but you gotta know what I want. You already know you're to step off on your left foot. Each step is thirty inches. You let your arms swing, elbows straight, twelve inches forward and six inches back of your center line.

"When you get the command to halt, you take one more step and then snap your heels together. 'Halt' can come on either foot and you stop on t'other foot. One, two.

"Every marching command happens on the next step. A command to turn will come on the foot in that direction – column left on your left foot, column right on your right foot. Then the move comes on the next step, so it comes on the other foot. The squad on the inside of the turn makes a full turn – on the ball o' your right foot to the left or t'other way. All the other squads make a half turn and then another half turn when you catch up. When you're headin' the correct way, you go to half-steps until your petty officer says 'forward march.' That'll make a lot more sense when we do it a few times.

"You turn around on the command 'To the rear, march.' The turn is to the right so it'll come on your right foot. You take the next step with your left foot and turn on the balls of both feet, then step off again on your left foot. I always get a few laughs out of this when you try it the first few times."

Fulton marched down the center aisle and executed "to the rear, HART" a couple of times in each direction. "When I say 'fall out,' go out to the street in front o' the barracks and fall in without a command. I want you in four ranks." Fulton looked at the recruits a moment. "Ryerson, Marshall, Downs and Carson. You look like the tallest men. You will start out as the squad leaders. Line up in that order, facing the building, and everyone else line up to their left. Stand at attention and silent. Got it?

"Fall OUT."

An hour later, they were lined up at the drinking fountain. "Well, that was a shambles," David said to Giovanni.

"Yeah, but I got some new words out of it. My little brother will be real impressed."

"I thought we'd be doing 'column right' and 'column left' until dark."

"That sumbitch was right, though. It was kinda funny, especially turnin' us around," Giovanni said. David smiled.

"Fall out for chow," Fulton shouted. The men scrambled out and fell into ranks. "We've improved a bit," David said to himself as they marched to the chow hall. "Still pretty motley."

They spent the evening after chow working on polishing their new shoes and pressing their clothes. David found himself coaching some of the men on using the iron.

"Everyone get a shower," Fulton said. "Cleanliness is next to Guardliness, I say."

The men got through the shower in groups, only about five minutes per group, and there was barely time to brush their teeth. "This is going to be a goat rope if we all try to shave in the morning," David said. "Let's just shave tonight." And this became a habit for the company.

"Nine o'clock. Everyone in the racks. Lights out," Fulton called.

"Dear God," David thought, "please bless us all..." He didn't realize he was asleep before his prayer was done.

The next morning began with a metallic clash. "Trash can lids for an alarm clock," David thought as he rolled from the rack.

"Hey, next time let me know you're comin' and I'll bake a cake," Giovanni said as David's feet tangled on the shorter man. "Tell ya what, you make a habit of comin' down at the foot and I'll get out at the head and maybe we won't collide."

"Get your clothes on and your racks made up," a voice shouted. It was a new petty officer. "I'm Fireman's Mate Caruthers. I'll be inspecting the bay in five minutes."

"Most of the rack mates are buddying up to help each other," David thought. "Couple of them aren't." Out loud he said, "I don't quite know how we're going to align the blankets at the heads."

Giovanni pointed to the bed frames. "Fulton didn't mention this – there are marks. Hey, guys, look at your frames. There are marks for the head blankets."

There was a flurry of shirts and shoes, blankets and pillows. "God, be with us. That's as much as I can think of just now," David prayed. "Couple of the men are kneeling for a moment – probably Catholics. Wonder how many are doing like I am, just praying as we go. Must be five minutes."

"Ten HUT." The company fell in at the heads of their racks by the center aisle. Caruthers was coming down the aisle.

"Somebody figured out the pillow covers. Smart work, that. You call this a rack?" He was speaking very loudly but not shouting. "You can try again." He pulled the blankets off the rack and piled them in the middle. Twice more he paused, looked with disdain at a recruit's rack and pulled the linens off of it.

"Shoes need work but I'll pay more attention to those tomorrow. All right, that'll do for your first inspection," he said after the offenders had remade their racks. "Still a lot of work to make coasties out of ya but it's a start. Fall out for chow!"

They assembled on the sidewalk in front of their barracks. The morning light was pleasant and the air cool. "This is the day You have made. Let us be glad and rejoice in it," David managed to say to himself as they stepped off.

No one was asking them what they wanted to eat as they came through the chow line. Their trays had divisions; scrambled eggs, bacon and toast went on every tray. "Too many of us to fry the eggs on request, I guess," David thought. "Or much else on request. They're feeding us like they sheared us yesterday – raw material more than young men." He sat at the long table next to the men who lined up to his left in formation. "For what we are about to receive, may You make us truly thankful," he said softly.

"Hey, go ahead and speak up," one of the other men said. "You seem like a dad type." The one who had spoken up did look even younger than most of the men in the company.

"For what we are about to receive, may You make us truly thankful," David said more firmly. "Me a Dad type? I turned eighteen in March."

"Well, I turned seventeen in July so you're a dad to me," the youngster said. "I'm Jason Priestly."

The two men across the table introduced themselves. "Mica Thorensen. I'm a lordly nineteen."

"Tom Sawyer and I've heard all the jokes. Well, I'm the old man here. I'm twenty-one and I can buy beer legally in any state."

"It's a good break, being first squad leader. You get to be first in the chow line," Jason said.

David smiled. "Some of the other lines, being first may be less of a good break." They all nodded.

They finished their meals quickly and carried their tableware to the clipper room. They formed up outside a few minutes later and Caruthers addressed them.

"We're headed over to get your shots now."

"First slot just became a losing proposition," David thought to himself as they marched several blocks. "Maybe I should be grateful for the immunizations, but I'm having trouble feeling grateful for the needles."

"Column of files from the left."

"Shirts off, recruits," a man in a white uniform ordered

"More stockyard than clinic," David thought. Men in white uniforms swabbed both of his arms and he received four injections in about thirty seconds. He moved outside. "Stand at ease, men," Caruthers kept saying as more men came into the formation. "Liable to pass out if you stand at attention right now. You men – sit down and put your heads on your knees." Two of the recruits were looking shaky and green around the gills.

"All right, we gotta wait here for fifteen minutes in case any of you get sick from the shots. Do you know the command 'Rest'? Means you can stand easy and even talk, just keep your places. Y'can only go to 'Rest' from 'Attention' and you only go from 'Rest' to 'Attention.' Right now we're hardly in formation. You're just all in one place."

Caruthers moved among the men, checking them as they came out, having some sit and put their heads on their knees if he thought they looked wobbly. About twenty minutes after the last man had come out, he moved to the front of the group. "All of you on your feet." He looked around.

"I guess we all look okay to him now," David thought.

"At my command – ten-HUT." Then he marched them back to their barracks.

Caruthers called them together toward the middle of the afternoon. "Stencils for marking your clothes," he said. "Anthony, Thomas. Arden, James." Each man received a couple of cardboard stencils with his last name and his initial, along with a bottle of white ink and one of black. "Black goes on your shirts, white on your pants," Caruthers told them. "Make 'em neat and clear."

A few evenings later, David was laying out his uniform for the next day and polishing his shoes with Giovanni. "It's been a blur," he said.

"That's about right," Giovanni said.

"I thought you were probably Catholic," David said.

"Oh, sure I am. We can't wear Christopher medals or anything like that during boot."

"Some of the other men have been kneeling, morning or evening, and I figured they were Catholics praying."

"Probably are. My family, we all kneel in church but we don't usually kneel at home. Fact is, we don't do a lot of praying at home either. We have the crucifix on the wall and the picture of the Virgin and everything else you think a Catholic home has. But I think it runs kind of shallow in our family. Dad's a factory guy and he's tired most of the time. Mama's got two grown up, me here, and three at home. So she's tired a lot too." Giovanni reached into his locker. "But even if it's a little shallow, it's still there. See?" He held up his rosary and a St. Christopher medal.

"Seems odd to me," David thought. "Those medals; I've been taught to think they're more superstition than religion. Religion...I was raised with God like I was raised to breathe or speak. Probably a good time to keep my thoughts private, though. Whatever his church, Giovanni is my friend and we all need all the friends we can get right now."

The next several days seemed to merge into each other. The morning inspections were often shambles – there were one or two men in each squad who drew most of the shouting, stripping, and tossing of clothes. Hours of drill. Classroom sessions about military law and customs. More hours of drill. In the barracks, constant cleaning of the bays and of their clothes.

"Captain of the head, David? That's sure a fancy name for the boot with the biggest target on his back."

David looked up ruefully from the toilet he was cleaning at one of his partners who was cleaning a shower. "Yes, Tom, the biggest target. If there's any job the instructors are watching more closely, it's this one. Keeping this place clean behind twenty men is a real chore. That midnight inspection and the – admonishment – from Fulton were annoying."

"Admonishment? That's a real nice term for 'ass-chewing.' Well, it'll help when more of the men understand how to keep it cleaner as they go."

David flushed the toilet and stepped to the next one. "I sure hope so." To himself: "This, too, is a prayer, dear God. This has to get done and You know we all hate doing it. 'Whatsoever you do...'"

A seaman with two stripes came to the barracks at eight o'clock on Sunday morning. "Catholics for chapel, fall out in front," he announced. Giovanni and about five other men went out. About an hour later, another seaman came. "Protestants for chapel, fall out in front," he announced. About half of the men went out front and joined a formation. They marched to the chapel and took their seats.

A distinguished-looking man in vestments stood in the pulpit. "I'm Father McManus, US Navy chaplain. I'm the only chaplain assigned here so I'm conducting services for all Christians. I'm also counselor and confessor for all Christians here at the training station. For that matter, I'll counsel with anyone. Denomination is less important than your souls. I say this every week before beginning the service because we're starting new men every week.

"This week is honorary Presbyterian week – we'll follow a common service order for that denomination. Next week will be Methodist. And so on.

"And let's begin with 'Amazing Grace' today, Number 47 in these hymnals."

David sang the hymn, sharing the hymnal with a boot from the third squad. "I don't know his name but his voice is very powerful," he thought. "Much better singer than I am."

The service continued. "Presbyterians order things differently from us Methodists," David thought. The chaplain was reading his text for the sermon. "I bet he uses the same text and sermon for both services," David thought. "It's hard enough to come up with a new sermon every week."

The text was from Matthew: "What think you? If a man have an hundred sheep, and one of them should go astray: doth he not leave the ninety and nine in the mountains, and go to seek that which is gone astray?"

"Your shipmates may go astray in a lot of ways. Here at boot camp, men will struggle with their chores and learning skills. Bring your shipmates along if you can. But you could be the one astray; if you're adrift, listen to your shipmates who are looking for you.

"It will be even more important at sea. The whole ship will stop for one man overboard. But there are other ways of being lost. It's strangely easy to be alone in the crowded berthing space. Every shipmate is part of your flock; even the shipmate who drives you crazy is of your flock.

"Maybe the hardest thing is when your shipmate is trying to get lost ashore. He may be drinking too much. He may be seeing women and telling himself it's love. And he's probably going to be angry if you call out for him, try to bring him back to the fold.

"The good shepherd seeks his lost sheep. Whether that's in action or on shore leave. And that lost sheep can be a stubborn cuss."

"Column of files from the left. Ford, HART."

David led his squad into the classroom and they formed up around tables with lengths of rope. Each position had ropes of different thicknesses and colors.

"We call ourselves coasties," their instructor said. "Coasties are also sailors and here's where you start learning about seamanship."

He called Giovanni into the center. "Ropes are a crucial part of every boat and ship," the instructor said. "A coastie has to know rope like he knows his own shoelaces. And the first thing he has to know is bights. Recruit, see that loop of rope on the floor?"

"Sir, yes sir."

"Any loop like this is called a bight. Put your foot in there." Giovanni stood as ordered. The instructor suddenly pulled on the rope and it seized up on Giovanni's ankle.

"We call that getting your foot in a bight." The instructor slackened the rope and Giovanni stepped out of it. "This was literal. As slang, getting your foot or your ass in a bight means getting into some kind of trouble. Sometimes it's called getting your ass in a sling.

"Now, think about a deck and loading cargo or handling small craft." David noticed that this instructor had a more – cultured, he found himself thinking – manner of speech than most of them had. "More like how I talk, anyway," he thought a bit wryly. "I wonder if he's felt out of place the way I sometimes do."

The instructor was continuing. "Lots of ropes around, lots of block and tackle, potentially a lot of bights. You can get any part of your body into a bight if you forget about them but you're most likely to get your foot in a bight on a deck. So always keep that in mind and watch how you place your feet. Watch how you place your ropes so you are less likely to get in a bight or to put a bight where someone else will get into it.

"This can be life or death, recruits. You take a heaving deck, put a man's foot in a bight and then someone takes up the slack or maybe the ship lurches, the least you can expect is a fall onto the deck and that can be bad enough. Depending on the load the line is handling, you can lose an arm or a leg this way. You can be tossed around and hit objects on the deck. You can be tossed overboard and drown."

"Sir, seems like there are a lot of ways to get killed in the Coast Guard besides the enemy shooting at us, sir," Giovanni said.

"You may think you're being funny but it's quite true. A ship's deck or a small boat is a dangerous place even on a quiet day. Get up a swell or a storm and it's that much more so. The Coast Guard's own ships are smaller and very handy, so they pitch and toss more than a lot of Navy ships do.

"We'll watch a film on knots and then we'll start working with them. The difference in the ropes' colors will help you understand some of the knots."

The instructor started the projector clattering and David watched closely. "I've tied some knots but just simple stuff," he thought. "This is the first time I've heard these terms: bight, fall piece, standing part.

"I've always heard of granny knots and thief knots but now I understand: they look square but they're weak. Strain will break them quickly."

After the film, they paired off at the tables and began to work. "Test each knot by pulling between you," the instructor said. "This time, tie a granny knot on purpose and test it. See it how it fails quickly." He came around for a particular demonstration: "If you need a small clove hitch, this is a nifty little trick that will impress your moms and dads when you get a leave." He showed them how to lay a line across the back of one hand and the palm of the other, then flick it into a clove hitch. "Obviously this is too small for a large post.

"One more trick to try with some of the knots. We usually pass the fall piece through. If you make a bight in the fall piece and pass the bight part way, you can make a lot of knots quick-release. You just tug on the end and it pops out. You can only use that sometimes."

They practiced the knots for about an hour. "You'll need a lot more practice, of course," the instructor said. "This is one of your key skills to graduate from boot camp."

"We've been here two weeks and this is our first chance out of the barracks on our own," Giovanni said.

"We have the vast space of this part of the post we can explore," David smiled. "I imagine the recreation hall is where things will be jumping."

"Hey, it's a relief to go anywhere without forty of our best friends at our side," Giovanni said. They headed over to the building.

"For a Podunk place, it's getting a lot of business," Giovanni said as they went in.

"Where else is there?"

"You play pool?"

"Yes," David said.

"See, I thought your idea of wild excitement was a Sunday service."

"My dad enjoyed pool sometimes," David answered. "He taught me the basics. And our church youth group had a pool table."

"Now, why did I figure you was a church youth boy?" Giovanni said. They sat down near one of the tables to wait for a turn.

"Yeah, you're better than I guessed," Giovanni said half an hour later. "I had to work pretty hard to beat you."

"Now you know why I didn't put up that dollar. But I'll spot you a Coke," David replied. He went to the vending machine, dropped a nickel and handed the cold bottle to Giovanni, then got one for himself.

David opened his Coke and they joined the men around the piano. A man from another company was playing jazz. One of the men in the group asked him, "Do you know 'Gee Mom'?"

"Gee mom, I want to go home?" the piano player asked.

"Yeah."

"Sure do." The player began a jaunty tune. "Let me discourse. The moving ballad, 'Gee, Mom, I Want to Go Home,' dates from just a short time ago. Our friends the Canucks gave it its first voice, but it is perhaps the most universally applicable song I have ever known. I gather, my learned friend, that you know some of it."

"Sure. I don't remember where I heard it. Maybe on a radio program."

The player continued to ripple the tune. "Some of the verses are pretty obvious and the song has a life of its own. You can add as many verses as you like. They can be as naughty as you like. And since all of our armed forces have names with two syllables, they all fit the tune to a T. Permit me to demonstrate.

"The coffee in the Coast Guard
They say is might fine.
It looks like Mississippi
And tastes like turpentine!

"Oh, I don't want no more of Coast Guard life!
Gee mom, I want to go,
But they won't let me go,
Gee mom, I want to go home!

"Our friends and brothers in arms, the Canucks, say they want to go back to Ontario, but as I said the song is universal. And no, they won't let you go."

The man who had proposed the song laughed with the piano player. "That's the one. Hey, guys, you can figure out how to sing along as we go. If you want to do a verse, raise your hand and I'll point at you so it's your turn. I'll do the next one. Maestro, if you please!

"The biscuits in the Coast Guard
They say are mighty fine.
One rolled off the table
And killed a pal of mine!
Oh, I don't want no more of Coast Guard life!
Gee mom, I want to go,
But they won't let me go,
Gee mom, I want to go home!"

James raised his hand.

"The women in the Coast Guard they say are might fine
They're built just like a barge is
And they look like Frankenstein!"

Everyone joined in the chorus. David smiled and sang along. Another man raised his hand and was recognized. "Got that one beat," the man said.

"The girls in the Coast Guard
They say are might fine!
Most are over ninety and
The rest are under nine!"

"Oh, the paychecks in the Coast Guard
They say are might fine.
They gave me forty dollars
And took back twenty-nine!"

David laughed and sang the chorus with the best of them. He sipped his Coke between verses. The men sang several other songs; eventually David drifted away. "I know we have to stay in the company area, but what I really want is to take a walk by myself," he told Giovanni.

"After two weeks of drill, my going-for-a-walk has about gone. But suit yourself. I'll see you back at the barracks."

The company area extended as far as the water on the south side. David strolled along the street, glad to be "at rest" as he walked. He walked up and down the sea wall. "Fresh breeze, sun bright, ocean softly murmuring. God, Your world goes on even when Your sons and daughters are making hash out of everything.

"I feel like I'm doing my best, God. I feel like You are sustaining me. All I've needed so far is fortitude – things have been annoying. If there are fearful or awful things, they're still ahead of me. Please stay with me, through boot camp and whatever is next. Especially whatever is next.

"Right now I'm only looking at the next day, the next task. Sufficient unto the day is the trouble thereof. I hope – I believe – there's a whole lot beyond boot camp, a whole lot beyond this war. For now, I'm grateful for what I need to get through day by day. Thank You."

Back in the barracks, David worked on a letter home. "I was glad to get your letter yesterday. Marianne, your paragraph at the end was so cheerful. And Dan, just seeing you signed it with everyone else means something.

"We'll have chapel services tomorrow and we have today and tomorrow off – as much as there are days off here at boot camp. We got to stay in bed until 6 instead of 5 in the morning.

"This week has been like last week -- drill, barracks, and how to live the Coast Guard life. We've started working with knots and ropes. You'd be amazed how many kinds of knots we are learning and how many kinds of ropes. Some of the men take it lightly but I can see how a strong knot, tied quickly, could mean the difference between life and death some day. God spare me it comes to that – but it probably will come to that sometime. We're coasties and coasties are sailors. Ships get into trouble all the time and then add a war.

"The company commanders push us around, the other instructors push us around, our squad leaders are boots and they push us around. I'm a squad leader and I have to push some of the men around. We are certainly on the first rung of the Coast Guard ladder and even the second rung seems like a long way up.

"I see this letter looks a lot like the one I sent last week. I have hopes that next week will be more interesting.

"Love to all. Yes, Dan, you too.

"David"

The next morning, Giovanni had an odd suggestion for David. "This week, you come to Mass with me and next week I'll go to chapel with you. Somethin' for both of us to learn."

"That seems kind of funny. I know Catholics are Christians, but I know some Methodists who would argue that point."

"My priest would argue whether Methodists are Christians. Maybe they need to go to each other's services more than you 'n me need to."

A chapel guide formed up the squad for Roman Catholic service. "I know your service is very different from mine," David said as they entered the chapel. "I don't want to make you look silly – or me."

"Just watch what I do."

"What about the Latin?"

"I get it a little more than some Catholics do because I speak Italian. But a lot of Irish and German Catholics get only a little of the Latin. There are two phrases you need: 'Dominus vobiscum' and 'et cum spiritu tuo.'"

"Et cum spirit two-two-oh?"

Giovanni laughed. "'Et cum spiritu … tuo.' It means 'and with your spirit.' It's the reply to 'Dominus vobiscum', which means 'The Lord be with you.' Mostly the priest says 'Dominus vobiscum' and we answer 'et cum spiritu tuo.' The Scripture readings will be in English and the sermon, too, so that'll be all right. You and me, we may have grown up in different churches, but we know it's one God."

David was already used to Father McManus's vestments. The incense was different and, of course, the conduct of the Mass in a foreign language. "And yet," David said to himself. "The order is a lot the same. I guess I should have expected that. The Methodist Church claims descent from the Anglican Church and so from the Catholic Church."

David found himself reading from the missal, kneeling when those around him did, and listening to the story of the Good Samaritan as the Gospel that day. "My favorite parable," he thought. But as he listened to the sermon, he got something new out of it. "All my life, I've thought the Samaritan was the good guy and he is. But I never knew the Samaritans were seen like Negroes."

The jangling of the bells during the Eucharist litany was a surprise but the consecration otherwise was the same that he was used to. Giovanni went with the other congregants for Communion but David stayed in the pew, kneeling.

"God, this I do know. It would be an insult to Giovanni if I took Communion as if I were a Catholic and I think my parents would be worried about it. One hour of Latin against a lifetime of teaching."

The next week, Giovanni was true to his word and attended the general Protestant service. They talked later as they shined their boots and brass.

"Well, the order of the service is a lot different from my Mass," Giovanni said.

"I don't know how the priest decided how to manage Protestant services. It's got to be kind of tricky. Most Protestant denominations accept each other's ministers easily but there's a lot of chafing between Catholics and Protestants."

"I was going to pass on Communion, just like you did, but it didn't come up."

"A lot of Protestant congregations only do Communion on first Sundays," David explained. "I guess it would be okay to take the Eucharist if it were blessed by a Catholic but I know a lot of Catholics won't take the Eucharist from a Protestant minister. I passed when I came to Mass with you because I thought it would be – well, almost an insult to the Catholics."

"They'd just have figured you were Catholic," Giovanni said.

"I would have known."

"That sea breeze is refreshing."

"Yeah, if refreshing means 'damn cold'," said Giovanni. "I like you making the best of everything you can, Dave, but four in the morning is a bad time to be cheerful. You ever get married, you wife might be grumpy about it."

David smiled anyway. "'This is the day that the Lord has made. Let us be glad and rejoice in it.' Half optimism, half sarcasm."

"All KP," the petty officer said. "Fall in. Right HAPE. Ford, HART." After a few paces, "At ease, HART." The six recruits all slumped a little. Even David found the early light and the dank breeze less inviting than he had at first.

"Ten-HUT! Column right, HART!" They made a turn, marched a short way further. "Halt!" They were outside one of the mess halls. Another petty officer in cook's garb was waiting for them. "The mess watch will take over. Dismiss."

"This way, lads. You don't have to use 'sir' with the mess watch." There were a number of men from other companies already in the mess hall. The cook detailed them around the various jobs. David and Giovanni found themselves in the pot-and-pan cleaning area. "I think we drew a short straw here," David said.

They hung their shirts on hooks and put on canvas aprons. Then they put on large rubber gloves. "That's a lot of pots and pans," Giovanni said as he looked at the conveyor.

"There'll be a lot more," said another of the recruits. "I was here last week. Failed a locker inspection and I'm back."

They ran huge sinks of hot water and detergent. "You'll wash 'em in the sinks, then spray them down to rinse. Then they go through the hot sanitizer. Watch out for that thing. It'll raise blisters even through those gloves. You'll change the water every thirty minutes."

"I guess I knew the pots and pans had to be huge," David said. "I mean, they're feeding a couple of hundred men three times a day." He put one of the enormous pots into the sink and got started.

Half an hour later, he looked at the conveyor. "It's just as full as when we started," he said to Giovanni.

"They keep cooking, you know. All damn day it'll be like this, I bet."

The KP veteran nodded. "Yeah, it will."

"Snap it up – more scrubbing and less talking," one of the cooks called over at them. "Change that water, remember."

"Why do we change the water like that?" the veteran asked.

The cook snorted. "You ever seen a whole company down with dysentery, boy? I have. That's why you change the water and that's why we steam the pots and all the dishes."

"I read about the Civil War. More men died from dysentery or measles or other camp diseases than died in battle," David said to his partners. "This is a lousy job, sure, but it's a lot more important than maybe you think it is. It'll be even more important aboard a ship."

"Yeah, sure," said Giovanni. "Meantime, keep scrubbing. I'm too busy for a history lesson."

"We're far enough ahead for you men to have your breakfast," one of the cooks told them. They herded into line and quickly ate their eggs, bacon and pancakes.

"This is the day that the Lord hath made," David said to himself a few minutes later as he resumed their task. "Sisyphean. I think I've got the rock up the hill and boom! We start all over." The room was steamy and their work kept them from chatting much. Scrub. Inspect. Over to the next sink. Scrub. Inspect. Scrub again.

"What happened with this one?" David said out loud.

"Yeah, that one is burned on. Hoist that over to this table. Here's some steel wool."

"Tough sheep," David said.

"Huh, recruit?"

"I thought it was a joke but I guess I was wrong," David replied. "Let me at it."

Ten minutes of tough scrubbing finally removed the crusted food. David carried the pot over to the sink and got back into the rhythm of the job. "Let's get you guys some lunch," another cook said.

"Lunch at 10:30? That's weird. But then we've been here six good hours already." Sandwiches this time and back to it.

Shortly after lunch, there was some grumbling among the recruits and they were moved around. David found himself working outside. The day had grown warm and humid. He and Giovanni were busy hosing and scrubbing trash cans. "Uncle Sam needs you," Giovanni said. "Damn recruiter didn't say why."

David looked up from his can and laughed. "Oh, my dad told me all about KP. An ancient military tradition."

"Well, my family didn't have any military tradition until me. And I don't plan to start no military tradition. Nobody told me about this."

"Maybe next time we'll be bashing spuds. That's the ultimate KP cliché, peeling potatoes."

Their last chore of the day was in the clipper room where table dishes came in. "Easier than the pots and pans," Giovanni said. They finished at around seven and one of their company petty officers marched them back to barracks. "All that hot water and now we need showers," David said. There were also piles of laundry on their racks; they finished the day by shining their boots.

"This morning was the first time we got past inspection with all the beds intact," David said.

"That'll win us the war," Giovanni said.

"And we're drilling like we mean it now also."

"Hey, today is going to be one of the most interesting days we'll get. We get to shoot rifles today."

The classroom had large posters of rifle sights and targets. Several targets with groupings in the bull's-eyes were posted on the walls. The instructor called them to order.

"You been learnin' a lot about your sea bag and livin' at sea. Started on some seamanship too – ropes and knots. Well and good, you need all that. But the Coast Guard comes from the Revenue Cutter Service. We was cops before we was doin' convoy and chasin' subs and we'll be cops when this war is over. Matter of fact, we're still cops, too. There are still crooks at sea, smugglers mostly and illegal aliens and all. Hard to believe but there are still pirates too.

"If I had my druthers, you'd all learn pistols as well as rifles. But we only got one day and we only got forty-eight rounds of each of you. So pay attention, boys. Learn it now 'cuz it'll be too late to figure it out when you need it. You'll get more with pistols if you get a job that needs it."

The instructor proceeded to discuss the basics of sighting and shooting. "You line up the sights just below what you want to hit. The rear sight is adjustable for elevation with this knob. We won't use it on the range today. If you're gonna need elevation, you'll get more training."

The next hour was a dull yet important lecture on safely handling the rifle and on principles of marksmanship. "It's hard to pay attention. I've been doing all this with Dad for years, but I'll have to do it the Coast Guard way today. God, please bring us all through today safely. Even on a range, something can go wrong."

There was a short break after the lecture. Several of the men got in a smoke around a butt can. David chatted with them but turned down the proffered cigarettes.

"All right, come over here and draw a rifle."

"Sir, a gun, sir?"

"In the Coast Guard, a gun is too big to pick up, recruit. These are rifles or weapons or firearms but they ain't guns. And if you'da said that to a Marine, you'da been sorry."

David and the rest of the company filed past a rack of Garand rifles and each man picked one up. An instructor at the end of the rack checked each weapon by making sure the safety was on, opening the bolt, locking it open and checking that there was no ammunition. "Muzzles high. Out to the firing line." The men filed onto the range and placed the rifles on the long counter. Each station had several clips and a box of ammunition.

"All right, then, turn around and watch the instructor in your section." The instructors were all old salts. Each had a rifle for demonstration.

"Here's the approved standin' position. Look at how you pull the rifle into your shoulder firmly. The M-1 kicks some and you'll beat yourself up 'less you hold it good and tight. Kinda like your favorite girl."

David grimaced. "I've never held a girl like that. But that's just like the Springfield 1903, easy enough." He had an odd twinge for a moment. "It's too bad I've never held a girl. Most of the men have."

"Set your feet about shoulder-width apart. Give yourself a good brace. Left hand forward under the forearm of the rifle.

"Now here's the kneelin' position." The instructor dropped to his right knee with his left elbow on his left knee. "See how he leans forward into his thigh and braces that elbow. This is almost as good a position as prone.

"Here's prone, now. Get around your instructor and see how he sets his legs an' his back. It ain't a straight line, ya see.

"All right, men. Each of you take your rifle and get into the standin' position. Your instructor will come around and coach you. Listen when he talks to the man next to ya; you can learn that way too, ya know."

The instructor came down the group near David. He adjusted elbows, used his foot to adjust the recruits' feet if necessary. He paused when he saw David.

"You done some shootin', son," the instructor said.

"Sir, yes, sir. I'm a hunter."

"A lot of the recruits are. Everybody can improve, son. Your stance is good and we'll sharpen it some." The instructor had David adjust his elbow, shift his position on the forearm. "That's pretty good." He went to the next man.

"Southpaw, eh? You done any shootin' before?"

"Sir, no, sir."

"Lotta southpaws are great marksmen but the weapons are all designed for right-handers. Well, you're better off with this semi-automatic than you'd be with a bolt action. But watch out for the brass. It'll be comin' right at your face. The clip, too."

They went through the same procedure with the kneeling and prone positions. So far they had only held the rifles. After each man had been coached in the three positions, David heard the order, "Ground your weapons. Instructors, make the line safe." He placed the rifle back on the bench and stepped back as the instructor came down the line and checked that each rifle was empty, action open.

"The line is safe. Instructors, take over for loadin' instructions."

"Come around me," the instructor said, moving to a position near the center of their section and placing some ammunition on the bench.

"This here is .30-06 jacketed ammunition. You load it in clips – these little metal holders and they hold eight rounds each. The clip goes in the magazine."

"Sir? Rounds?" a recruit asked. The instructor looked amused.

"A loaded cartridge is a round. You can call it a cartridge if you want, but it ain't a bullet. The bullet is the business end of the round or cartridge.

"Now you put eight rounds in each clip, like this." He showed them how to load the clip. "You push the loaded clip into the magazine from the top." He demonstrated. "A lot like loading the 1903, but the whole load goes in at once," David told himself.

"Now the bolt wants to pick up that first round but you don't want that right now. So you start to close the bolt while you're pressin' down on the top round with your left thumb. Or cartridge, but it ain't a bullet." The instructor was holding the operating rod with his right hand. "When you're loadin', you gotta keep good control of the operatin' handle with your right hand. See where your thumb is in the bolt? You let that handle go when your thumb is in the way and you'll get what we call M-1 thumb. Hurts like hell. So you gotta watch your hand any time you're workin' with the operatin' handle but that's usually when you're loadin' or unloadin'."

"I bet it hurts like the very mischief," David said to himself. The instructor had let the bolt close.

"Now here we're loaded but the chamber is empty. You use the operatin' handle to charge the bolt – you draw it back an' let it go forward and it chambers the top round." He demonstrated. "When you've emptied the clip, it'll pop out of the action on its own and the bolt will lock open. Then you just put in a new clip, close the bolt and keep shootin'.

"You unload about like you'd think. Open the bolt with the operatin' rod and pull back until it locks. See how I keep my left hand over the bolt to catch the round that's ejectin'. I loaded without a round in the chamber, so there wasn't one to eject. You release the magazine with this knob. Then I close the bolt with th' operatin' rod, watchin' out for M1 thumb.

"You'll hear a command, 'Lock and Load.' That means you check your safety is on, you load a clip into the magazine, and you let the action load that first cartridge. The rifle is ready to fire when you take off the safety."

"Sir, in battery, sir?" David asked.

"That's the fancy way to say it, yep. In battery. Once it's in battery, you make sure you keep your safety on until you're ready to shoot somethin'. Or maybe somebody. And always know where your muzzle is pointin' 'cuz I'll take it personal if you point it at me.

"Be careful, here, boys. If you let the bolt close, it'll chamber the top round and then you're ready to shoot. Always know whether you got a round in the chamber – in battery, as your shipmate said." The instructor demonstrated again.

David raised his hand and the instructor called on him. "Sir? It looks like you wouldn't really load single rounds, sir," he said.

"Good catch there, recruit. It's possible but it's doin' things the hard way. You carry the ammo in the clips and you rarely have loose rounds to top up with."

"All right, go to your stations and load your clips with eight rounds."

David loaded his clips. There were enough cartridges for six full clips.

They started with the prone position. "Take your sights. Fire when ready."

There was a rattling volley. David squeezed his shot and looked down range. Spotters were holding up the cards to indicate each shooter's result. "Couple of Maggie's Drawers," the instructor said. He went down the line to coach each shooter. "You was just a little bit high," he said when he saw the card. David nodded.

"All right. Take your sights. Fire when ready." David kept the same sight picture but eased the trigger a little more carefully. The ragged volley, the cards went up. "Ya got a bull's-eye," the instructor said. "Maggie's Drawers again, son," to the shooter next to David. He coached the shooter briefly about sight picture and about flinching.

They continued to fire through the positions. At the end, they carried their rifles into a shed to clean them. As they were cleaning them, the instructor came in. "Ryerson, you was top shooter for our squad. Forty-four in the bull's-eye and four in the 9 ring. Good work, son."

Giovanni was running the patch rod down his barrel. "That was probably the most fun thing we'll do here," he said.

"It was fun on the range. God send that we only ever need these on the range," David said. "I know how I'd shoot a man. I don't know if I can."

"All right, all hands. Make sure you hit the head before we get into the boat. We'll be out an hour or so and this is the last chance you'll get."

A few minutes later they were beside the boat.

"Your first test is getting into the surf boat. Find your place. Pass your oars and stand by. Keep your body low and you're less likely to get wet."

David clambered into the boat. "Keep three contact points. Keep moving; someone is coming behind you. Scramble forward and get set. It sure rocks. Second seat forward, on the left. All right, I'm squared away. Get the rowlocks in place." He rigged his gear as their instructor had told them. Jack was having a hard time. "Hey, give me a moment and I'll bear a hand." Now all but two of the men were seated and the instructor was at the tiller. Marcus was at the bow and Travis was at the stern with the ropes that held the boat at the dock.

"Cast off the painter. You at the bow. The front, you landlubber. You oughtta know the bow from the stern by now." Marcus looped his rope off of the cleat and stepped into the boat, getting into the first seat.

"You, cast off the stern line." Travis looped his rope off the cleat and got in at the stern. "Stand by your oars.

"Refresher course. You recruits on this side ..." he gestured with his right hand "...are on the starboard. It feels strange because you're facin' aft, but your left is starboard right now. So that makes you men..." he gestured with his left hand "...the what?"

"The port, skipper?"

"Yeah, the port, and two points for using 'skipper.'" The boat had drifted slightly from the dock. "Shove off, port side. Give it a good push. Now haul in the fenders. Ship oars." They pulled in the two fenders, oblong knots of rope that cushioned the boat's hull against the dock. Then they got their oars into the locks and ready to row. "Couple of near-scalpings," David smiled to himself.

"All right, when there's more pull on the port side of the boat, the boat will head starboard. Or if there's drag on the starboard, the boat will turn that way. Likewise to the port. My rudder can provide the drag that will turn the boat.

"You have to have way on a boat to control it. Here we are, just floating. I'm working the tiller and the rudder and all I'm doing is wobbling the boat. I can get just a little way on like this. If a boat has any way on – rowed, motor, towed – you can steer it.

"The command to row is 'give way.' You'll have to work as a team with two parts – port side and starboard. Everyone has to pull about evenly unless I tell one side 'oars' or 'back water.' If the port side is rowin' normal and the starboard stops or backs, the boat'll spin to starboard very sharply. Maybe too sharply; you can swamp a boat or capsize it that way.

"Stand by. Give way together easy." All of the men dipped their oars and pulled mightily. They brought their oars back for the next stroke. "That's a face full of water," David thought. "Lot of us got one."

"Takes a while to learn rhythm, men. Now, 'easy' means slowly and 'handsomely' means just a little faster. 'Cheerily' means to go briskly and 'smartly' means get right to it. Stand by, all together, give way easy." The boat staggered forward and a little to starboard. "Port side is getting more into their oars," David thought.

Their instructor was more patient than the company commander had been at drill, though. "Only way to learn this is to do it, men. It's a lot like marching. You had to learn to take the same steps and now you have to learn to take the same strokes. Have to work as a unit."

A few minutes later they were moving the boat more steadily. "We're catching on," David thought. "It's a bright day, dear God, getting warm. And thank You for a quiet sea to get us started."

"Well that. Oars! Keep them level, just like the squad in formation. I'll call stroke this time to help you get rhythm and get the pace I want. Give way together, handsomely. Stroke! Stroke!"

"The cadence is certainly helping," David thought.

"Oars! Well that. Port side, give way easy. See how the boat turns like this. Oars. Starboard side, give way easy. Oars. See? Same thing.

"Listen for this command. I want the starboard men to give way and the port men to back. Stand by – stroke!" The boat spun quickly. "Oars."

The lesson continued for about an hour, as the instructor had said. "We must have gotten – oh, about a hundred yards from the dock," Giovanni said.

"Probably just as well for a first day," David replied.

"We'll be doin' a lot of that," Giovanni said. "I'm almost as wet as if I'd fallen in. How are your hands, David?"

They compared their palms. They were reddened but not blistered. "They'll toughen up," David said. "Between knot practice and rowing, we'll get some good callouses."

"We'll need 'em," Giovanni said.

David was working on a letter a couple of evenings later. "We're doing more with the boats and we're looking better. Some of the men seem to be working harder at it than others, I have to admit. It just startles me that anyone would be slacking off. We're here to learn and we all depend on each other – if the head is dirty or the formation is awkward, we all pay for it. It's even more true in the surf boat – there are ten of us literally in the same boat. We depend on each other for our lives and a few of the men still seem to scamp their share. Maybe they still have to figure out that we depend on each other as much as we do.

"We've been learning hand-to-hand fighting as well. Our instructors are Negro boxers. They're teaching us a lot more than boxing, though. It's a good thing the gloves are thick and we have other padding on. One of the instructors put it well: if we have to use these skills, it'll be in a mix-up and we'll be fighting for our very lives. So I'm paying close attention even though I hope I'll never need these skills.

"We pair up by size in fighting class, but once in a while the instructors mix us up. Giovanni might have to fight someone my size and I may have to fight someone his size, the instructors say, and I was surprised at how difficult it was to fight someone smaller than me and who really meant to get me down! In the end, I did grapple Giovanni and pin him. But he had gotten in quite a few licks before that! He told me he'd done a lot of scrapping in his neighborhood. This is the first sparring I've done in my life.

"This week made for a much more interesting letter than last week – now that we're moving past drill and barracks duty and learning more about being sailors and even fighting. Keep writing, please keep writing. If you think hearing about the same stuff every week is boring, put that idea away. We're learning to serve our country so we can protect that same stuff every week.

"I was surprised to get a letter from Andrea Matthews this week. She said that Pastor Dan had suggested she write. She said she'd gotten started in secretarial school. She even sent me a picture, which was nice of her. I'm having a hard time with the guys; they all assume she's my girlfriend, instead of just a friend I've grown up with in church. Her brother Walter was drafted and he's at Ft. Dix for Army boot camp.

"Lights out in a few minutes. God be with you all.

"Love, David."

"Well, we're in our Sunday best now," Giovanni said. "First time we've been allowed to wear our blues for chapel."

"Last Sunday at boot camp. We get our assignments tomorrow and graduation parade is on Tuesday," David said. "Wednesday we scatter."

"The Coast Guard giveth and the Coast Guard taketh away," Giovanni said. "I'm off to Mass. I'll see you at lunch, then. You look good in the blue jumper but it feels kind of silly."

David laughed. "Well, it's a traditional outfit. Our workday clothes are more like what we'd wear as civilians."

"If we were civilians in jail. Hey, I'm still a civilian at heart," Giovanni replied. "At least at our next postings we can get passes."

"Civilians at heart," David repeated. To himself: "Less so than you may think, friend Giovanni. The recruiter said different men would go home than the boys who came here. And even six weeks has been enough to show he's right."

"My last service with Father McManus," David thought as he took a seat. "And it's Eucharist Sunday as well. That's the note I'd choose to end boot camp."

The chaplain began his text. "Blessed are the meek, for they shall inherit the earth." Then he began in earnest.

"That's a whole new take," David thought.

"Some of you are just starting boot camp but I want to speak to the men who graduate this week. 'Blessed are the meek,' you have heard all of your lives. The next months, maybe the next years, of your lives are going to make meekness a real challenge. You must become skillful in the crafts that the Coast Guard will teach you. You must be obedient and you must also require others to be obedient. You must have confidence in yourself and in your shipmates, especially the man who will be on your left and the man on your right. You must believe in the cause for which you have set aside all your plans before the war.

"And withal you must still be meek. It is very difficult to look up from a task well-done and say to yourself, 'God's glory and not mine.' It is very difficult to go into action against the enemy, to emerge victorious and think 'Jesus brought us through.' You will think, and think rightly, that your skill and your commitment, your teammates' skill and commitment, brought you through the crisis and will bring you through the next crisis.

"William Shakespeare gets very little pulpit time, but he should get more. In 'Henry V', Shakespeare has King Henry telling his army that they must give God the glory for their victory at Agincourt and not boast of it. I like the sentiment even if I doubt the real king was that humble.

"I want you to remember always that it is the love of Jesus that gives you your skill, the love of Jesus that gives you your commitment. It is the love of Jesus that gives you a mission in this war."

The chaplain smiled. "To your good fortune, the Coast Guard has thousands of ways to help you stay meek. Your section leaders will remind you of your places. Your quarters will be austere. Between the exciting tasks of gunnery or rescue, there will be many tasks like chipping paint and cleaning heads. When I was your age, I found that KP was very effective at keeping me meek."

Ten minutes later, David lined up for the Eucharist. A few minutes after that, he was leaving the chapel. "Chaplain, that was surely a different approach to blessing the meek, sir," he said as he shook the chaplain's hand. "I hope I can hold onto it."

"Are you graduating this week, son?"

"Sir, yes, sir."

"Will your parents be able to come for the parade?"

"No, sir."

The chaplain took him into an embrace. "I'll stand in for your earthly parents for a moment, son, and ask the Trinity's blessings for you."

The chaplain asked each boot who paused to chat if he was graduating and blessed each of them in the same way if the boot said his parents would not be at graduation. Only a few expected their parents.

The last training day began with a formation for the eagerly-awaited assignments. "Anderson, cutter Comanche. Bailey, radio school. Gunther, transport Samuel Chase. Paulsen, radio school." David came to attention. "Ryerson, landing craft school. Zirilli, cutter Spencer."

"Well, how you rate, David!" Giovanni laughed. "You get a few more months ashore and I'm headed right to sea."

Monday evening they checked each other's uniforms and brass. "We'll make fine figures tomorrow," David said.

"I'm glad my parents can make it," Giovanni answered.

At the end of Tuesday's parade, the boots were allowed to mingle with the guests. "Giovanni, we're so proud of you!" his mother said.

"Mom, Dad, this is David Ryerson. The long drink of water I wrote to you about," Giovanni said. David shook hands with Giovanni's father first. "I'm glad to have known your son, Mr. Zirilli," he said. "We've helped each other through this."

Giovanni's mother only let him get as far as "Mrs. Zirilli..." before she had pulled him down to her. "Your momma can't be here, boy," she said. "So I'll be your momma for a minute."

David laughed. "It's almost worth missing my mom and dad, to have so many moms and dads standing in for them," he said.

Wednesday morning was a flurry of last-minute packing into sea bags and footlockers, stripping the beds and giving the barracks a last touch-up. "Another company will be here tonight or tomorrow. God be with them."

Giovanni was scheduled for a bus to a train station at 7:30; David's bus to the training center was to leave an hour later. "Well, the two boys who met on Day One are now the seamen parting after six weeks," David said.

"Seamen! We're seamen like we're men – just getting started."

"Giovanni, whatever is waiting for us, we're probably saying our last good-by. Our only good-by. I'll try to pray for you every day. I hope you'll pray for me. Dominus vobiscum."

Giovanni held his hand. "I can see this Italian is kind of embarrassed but glad as well," David thought.

"Et cum spiritu tuo, David. I pray Jesus gets us both through this." And Giovanni shouldered his bag, struggled a moment to lift his footlocker, and was gone.

New River

"Long ride," David thought as their bus rolled south. "We've passed through cities and towns and farms and farms and farms. And now it's gotten too dark to read. I should take the examples of my shipmates and sleep a while." He settled into a thin doze as the bus rolled on.

"Hm. Three in the morning. We're entering a post. Marine Barracks New River welcomes us, the sign says.

"MP boarding the bus. Wants to see everyone's ID cards." David got his from his wallet and held it up for the cursory inspection.

A few minutes later they were stopped at a squat brick building. A CPO came aboard the bus and said, "All out. Here's your new home, coasties."

They draggled into the barracks with their gear. "Racks already made," David thought. "A rare courtesy!"

The chief was speaking as they began stowing their gear. "I'm Chief Bosun's Mate Rockwood. This is a Marine Corps post but you are coasties, not gyrenes. We'll be working alongside them and the Army, naturally. You have to learn to drive these boats and the infantry has to learn to use them. We'll talk about that in the morning, after chow, when you're awake and so am I."

The men sacked out quickly. Only a few hours later, the dorm guard was clattering the trash can lids and they were getting ready to start their first day.

"There are men from a couple of different companies at Manhattan Beach," David realized as they shaved and squared away their quarters. "Some from other boot camps, too."

The chief assembled them in the bay right after breakfast. "You're done with boot camp. We figure you got through that and you can start acting like real coasties. You'll have base liberty and even get passes into town once in a while. There will still be drill and PT, still be fatigue duty and KP and all the fun you're used to now, but that's because things have to be done. You still need to look sharp and take care of your barracks. And you're still becoming coasties.

"You only need to call officers 'sir' or 'ma'am' here and there are just as few ma'ams here as there were at boot. So if you're thinking about one of those Great War movie romances, you'll have to look off-post.

"I said last night we'd be working with gyrenes and doughboys. It's our job to get 'em to the beach and their job to keep going inland. Both jobs are plenty tough.

You call the Army and Marine officers 'sir.' You can call anyone with two stripes or less 'Marine' or 'soldier' or 'buddy' but anyone with three stripes or more is 'sergeant.' Their NCOs hate to be called 'sir.' A few of the infantry will remember to call you 'coasties' but most of them will call you 'sailor.' Just let it go. They mean it kindly.

"Now you need to get along with the Marines and Army while we're here. The polite reason is that we're all in this war as a team. Another reason is that Marines are taught to think they're mighty tough and some of them like to prove it. Damn few of you are likely to come out ahead in a brawl with the Marines or even Army and I want you to stay out of trouble. I've got better things to do than to get you out of the brig or pick you up at the hospital. And the skipper will give you hell at captain's mast if you make trouble.

"That's enough to get you started with making friends here. Fall in in five minutes out front and we'll start your real business."

"Squad leader again," David thought a few minutes later, after they had sorted by size. "The curse of being taller than most of the guys." They marched to their classroom near the piers. "Look at all those ships," David thought. "And boats to go with them"

A gruff, older-looking petty officer was their instructor for the day. "Boatswain's Mate First Class Yarnell. You can call me 'bosun.' Recalled six months ago to try to teach you something about small craft. Nobody has years of experience with these ramped boats; they're a brand-new idea. But I've had my own run through the training program and I've pushed boats that are handy and clumsy for a long time.

"You're going to learn to run these boats by running these boats, but there are a lot of things you'll learn faster if we tell you about them first. That's what these movies are going to be about. When we get onto the boats tomorrow, I expect you to remember and use the information in the movies."

Bosun Yarnell drew the curtains and the projector began clacking. David watched intently. "That music is less stirring than they think it is. Transom. Emergency rudder access – yeah, I bet you might need that. Ramp controls. Gun mounts." The film went on – more engagingly than David had expected. "And I'm going to need to know all of this."

"Skeg. Helps keep the rudder and the propeller out of the sand." The metal rod seemed oddly flimsy to serve so crucial a purpose. "If the boat tilts a little to left or right, seems like the prop or the rudder would still foul. Maybe the flat bottom helps prevent that kind of tilting. The boat's designed to be pretty flat on the beach, after all.

"Bow ramp winch – hand-cranked, I thought it would be electric. Takes two men to raise it. Stow the handle when the ramp is up – yeah, it would beat you up pretty badly if it was on that gear when the ramp was coming down.

"A place for everything and it had better be there. Sure. If you leave your gear loose, it'll go flying around. And everything has to be in the right place or somebody who has to jump into the job will have a hard time finding it.

"Maneuvering. Hey, I missed that before." The film's narrator was describing how the rudder's action turned the stern of the boat and that was how the boat's direction changed. "You steer by skidding, really, not by pointing the bow. Not like the Buick at all! I should have figured that out before.

"You've got to back the boat off a beach. It backs very awkwardly – have to watch that. I hope we practice that a lot. Come to think of it, I'll probably be very tired of how many times we'll practice that."

"Broaching lines. Attached to the stern, handled by the shore party to help you keep the boat backing straight out to sea. If it starts to swing parallel to the beach, the line party will try to pull the stern against the motion of the broaching.

"Rudder action is weak when backing. Need to keep that in mind. Getting off the beach is a lot trickier than getting onto it."

"The gang seem quietly excited tonight," David thought in the barracks. He was reading "Two Years Before the Mast." "We have a big day tomorrow, first day in the boats. There are George and Harry, at it again. Wig-wagging naughty words. Well, whatever helps them learn."

Ten of them went aboard the LCVP the next morning. "I'm Boatswain's Mate Second Class Cleaver. Seaman First North is my engineer. Call me 'bosun' or 'coxswain.' You all know something about small craft, of course. These boats tend to be clumsy rather than yar."

"'Yar', bosun?" David asked.

"Okay, I'm an old salt. 'Yar' is a term for a boat or a ship that handles easily, sometimes too easily. Chop-and-change artists, like speedboats and cutters. With a good crew, a surf boat is very yar. They usually have narrow beams and powerful engines."

"Our instructor at Manhattan Beach used the term 'handy.'"

"Yep, means about the same thing. What are some things you know about these boats that would tend to make them more awkward than, say, a surf boat?"

George spoke up. "They're broad in the beam."

"That's one thing. There are two other characteristics that make them sluggish or awkward."

"Their hulls are much less tapered at the bow and stern," David replied.

"That's right. One more, boys." There was some mumbling but no one seemed to have an answer. "They're shallow in the draft and that makes them more responsive to current and wind."

"Leeway, bosun?"

"Yes, leeway. Every vessel makes some leeway. You have to learn to work with leeway because it's like gravity – it's always there."

"We're lucky today," David thought as he looked at the bay. "Quiet as a mill pond. Mild autumn day, wind light. It's as warm here as early September would be at home. Our first experience will be pretty easy."

"Everybody has to know every job," the instructor was saying. "You'll kind of work your way up – bowman and stern man, engineer, coxswain. The men who have a particular mechanical bend may specialize as engineers. The ones who show leadership and boat-handling skills will be coxswains. That doesn't take anything away from the bowmen and the stern men, though. Probably all of you will have your own boats within a year or so."

"Why is that, bosun?" Harry asked.

"We're building a lot of these boats. Mr. Higgins has his boys hopping all day, every day. After you've had a few landings, you'll be needed as the experienced men to work with the new men. Some of you may even come back here as instructors."

"And because some of us aren't going to make it," David thought to himself.

The coxswain did a tour of the boat. "Ramp dogs here. Watch these cables that raise the ramp; get your hand in there and you could be Lefty for the rest of your life. Machine gun tubs but we won't use them. Bilge. Lockers. Lotta rope in different sizes. Semaphore flags. Helm. Engine station."

He started the engine. The Gray Marine diesel rumbled. "Watch your instruments when you've got the engineer's slot, men. These are highly reliable engines, tough as can be, but they need your attention. The coxsun needs to be aware of the engine, too, but it's the engineer's job."

"Kinda stinky," one of the men said.

"I'm so used to it that I like it," Yarnell said. "Here's the helm. The coxswain revs the engine with the throttle here, engages the propeller here. The wheel is flat and you can raise it or lower it here.

"Ryerson, cast off the stern line. Mack, stand by the painter. See how I engage just a little forward power and I turn the wheel into the dock. That pushes the stern away. Cast off the painter, Mack." David had nipped aboard as soon as he'd cast off the stern line and now Mack stepped aboard.

"I'll reverse a minute here. All right, got some clearance. Engine in neutral. See how the wheel doesn't do a thing right now – you have to have way on to have steerage." Yarnell engaged forward and increased the speed a little. "Now we've got way on and the boat responds to the helm." He motored along for a few minutes. "I don't know any of you from Adam, so you're each going to take a turn at the helm in alphabetical order. Sort yourselves out. You'll watch the engines for a few minutes, then have a turn at the wheel. I'll be right here to keep things moving and to keep things from getting too lively. Got a long day."

"Bosun, what about the head?"

"You can see that the accommodation is sketchy, son. I hope you only have to take a leak. Be sure you're on the leeward side when you do it. Same thing if any of you need to puke."

"Puke? On a day like this?" David asked. It seemed more like a lark than training.

"Well, son, some people do. And some of you are likely to shake your shipmates up when you're learning to drive these boats. When we take them out in real weather, you may all need to puke. Even I do, once in a while."

"Allison, Baker, Galileo – really? – Henderson, Kelly, Marino, Ryerson, Taylor, Vincent, Yeager. Allison, you stand here at the wheel. Kinda tight, yeah. Baker, you there with North to watch the engine. Everyone else just keep an eye on things."

There were several boats, LCVPs and LCMs, on the bay. "All of these boats are like us, first day in the boat or just a few days in the boat. So everyone keep your eyes skinned. It's easy for us to get in each other's way and the skipper gets peevish if we even scrape the paint. Allison, take the helm." A tall young man with a confident air stood at the helm and took the wheel.

"See the tower yonder. Make for that and open up the throttle a little." They motored for five minutes or so, steady as a rock. "Now, see how we're making leeway to the east. What would you do about that?"

"Aim a little west and adjust as we go, maybe put on a few more turns to make up for seaway we've already lost."

"That's right. You have to learn to judge that. How much have you been in small boats, Allison?"

"All my life, bosun. Father's a fisherman in South Carolina."

"So you're almost home here."

Each coastie got a ten-minute turn to start. Some handled the boat confidently, others appeared rigid and waited for the bosun to tell them everything they should do. David found himself crouched by North, the engineer, listening to a shouted introduction to the engines. "Oil pressure, water temperatures, RPM. These are great engines as long as you mind them. Here's the brake for the landing ramp and the winch to crank it back up." Then it was David's turn at the helm.

"What's your experience with boats, son?" Yarnell asked.

"Rowboats, small outboards, then boot camp," David said as he took the wheel. "This wheel seems odd, flat like this."

"We've all had to get used to that. Quite a change from a tiller or from the wheels on most craft, yeah. Here's your throttle and your forward-reverse control. You rev up to a speed you like and the throttle will hold it. You don't have to keep riding it like you do the gas pedal on a car. See the end of that island to the west? Make for that and allow for some leeway east."

After the next man took the wheel, David went to the lee side. "Something else to get used to," he thought. "Tinkling over the side like this. It feels awfully public but it's just us out here after all."

The next demonstration turned out to be quite interesting. "Maybe you thought you had to be on a beach to lower the ramp. It's hard tell from in here, but the lower edge of the ramp is above the waterline – with this load, well above the waterline. That means you can lower the ramp any time you might need to. More important, you can pull off a beach while you're raising the ramp if you need to and you won't flood your boat. North, get on the brake. You two, undog the ramp. North, let it down a foot or two." The engineer released and then clamped the brake and the bow ramp lowered.

"Okay, we're going pretty slowly, only four or five knots. A slow speed for a man who's running. There's very little sea right now – that's why we start in this bay, it takes a lot to make it choppy. See how a little water comes into the deck like this. Goes down in the bilge to be pumped out later.

"Now I'll open up the throttle some. A lot more water coming in now. Ryerson, tail onto the winch with North and raise the ramp. You men dog it. You two, man the pump and clear us out.

"If you're having to clear a beach because there's another boat right behind you, and there will be another boat behind you, then you can raise the ramp while you're retracting and you can even make your turn while you're still raising the ramp. The boat will handle even with the ramp all the way down. , but the faster you're going or the lower the ramp is, the more water you'll ship. If the ramp is all the way down, the boat will be a lot more awkward and it can ship a lot more water."

"Seems like how much water you ship would depend a lot on how high the sea is running," Galileo said.

"You're right about that – a high sea will make you ship a lot more water. There's something else that might make you want to skedaddle and worry about the ramp in a minute though."

"What's that, bosun?"

"Maybe somebody is shooting at you. Or maybe somebody shot you up already and the ramp is stuck down."

They motored around the bay for several hours, each coastie taking turns at the different positions. They had the ramp up and down several times, pumped out repeatedly. Finally they tied up the Papa boat and cleaned it thoroughly.

"We're a tired, motley crew heading for chow," David thought as they marched from the dock to the mess hall. "Kinda damp, too. There was a fair amount of spray and wash."

In the barracks that night, David and George practiced Morse with their flashlights. "Bible verses, David? How about something more fun?" George said.

"All right," David said. He flashed, "What is the last note a bee hums?"

George laughed and flashed, "Okay, what?"

"Beeee flat."

"I'll admit I think little enough of the film I'm about to show you," Bosun Yarnell said. "You boys are getting your first liberties to town this weekend and I have to tell you something about venereal diseases."

There was a lot of guffawing. "Some of us may know more than you think about VD," one of the rougher men said.

"I'm sure some of you do," Yarnell said. "But I'll ask you if I want your opinion or help. It's a fact that there's a lot of VD running around New River and coasties are hardly immune. Getting laid here is like Russian roulette with your pecker."

"That's half an hour of my life I want back," one of the men said as they took a break.

"I don't know what to think of that," David said to himself. "But this is part of what Pastor Dan was telling me about."

After chow that evening, David put on his blues. Half of the men in the barracks had passes that evening, good for the weekend if they wanted to stay off post that long and had the money. "Lucky cuss," a couple of men were chaffing a friend. "Got your wife in town!"

"Sure do," he said. "I just wish I had a little more money for a decent room."

David and a couple of others found singles. "Show her a good time," one of them insisted when the coastie tried to demur. In the end, he accepted the small gift with a smile. "It's been a long time and I did want to go somewhere nice," he said as he left with his overnight bag.

"God, please bless him and his wife tonight," David thought. "Please help them enjoy an experience I've never had."

David and a couple of others caught a base bus to the gate, then a city bus into town. "We'll start with a brew," O'Malley said. They went into the first bar. "All of you eighteen?" a doorman asked.

"Yes, sir," each of them answered. He didn't check their cards. They took a table and a waitress came over. "Beer all round?" she asked. Ben and Mark nodded.

"Could I have a coke, please, miss?" David said.

"Sure enough, coastie. You boys want sandwiches too?"

"What have you got?"

"Just ham and cheese; we ain't rightly a restaurant. But I make 'em myself and I put a little love on each of 'em." She smiled at them and headed to the back.

They toasted with the drinks when she brought them: "To our first pass! And many more!"

"Can we run a tab, ma'am?" Ben asked.

"Sorry, honey, we've had too many boys on pass in here for that. Some of your friends has lost track as they was enjoyin' themselves, they was short when it was time to pay. Pay as you go." She brought their sandwiches a few minutes later. They were thick and tasty. "But where's the love?" one of them asked.

"We'll just have to believe her," David said. "A nice girl like that would only tell us the truth."

"Heh. You should'a paid more attention to the VD film," Ben said.

"I'd sure rather be at home," Ben said. "When I get a leave, Rita and I are going to have a real time. I may get to my ship broke."

"You figure we're going to ships?"

"That's the whole point of this school. Of course we're going to ships. Then to who knows where? Any place the Nazis and the Japs are holding on and there's a beach that infantry can cross. And I'm betting the Nazis and the Japs have got the welcome mats ready for us. But let's talk about home. Who did you leave behind, Dave?"

David smiled. "Mom and Dad, a bratty brother, a princess sister and an old cat."

"No girl?"

"Nope. Never have had a girlfriend. I hope to fix that some day."

"Tall, smooth talker, good looking. There's probably a church full of girls been willing to fix that."

David laughed. "Why did you say 'church'?"

"Because you ordered a coke instead of a beer. This is our first chance at a drink off-base in a long time. Only church boys order cokes in a bar on pass."

"Something wrong with that?" David was bristling slightly.

"Oh, gosh, I see how that sounded now. More respect than laughin' at you, Dave."

"I did take it wrong," David replied. They shook hands.

The waitress appeared again. David was still nursing his coke but the beers were gone. "How about we each give you a dollar and you tell us when we've used it up?" Ben asked.

"That'll work, boys. But you keep your heads on you. This is a nice joint and we don't want a fight or nothin'. And sometimes the rowdies come around when it gets late, think you boys are easy pickins."

"Fights? Why would they want to fight us?"

"Because they're rowdies but mostly because they think they can rob you."

Mark laughed. "If we've had a good time with you, there won't be much to take us for."

"True enough, honey," she smiled. Then she was serious a moment. "But they've busted up some o' the men on pass pretty bad. Even a couple of Marines. The rowdies come sober and lookin' for drunks."

The conversation covered a lot of territory: family and women, their instructors, women, the course of the war to date, women, small boats, women, the likely length of the war and women. "I'm a little on the outside," David thought on his third coke. He had enjoyed his sandwich and their waitress had kept a bowl of chips filled for them. She brought another round and said, "That's all, boys, unless you want to chip in some more money."

David looked at his friends. "Buzzed," he thought. "Not really drunk. Just enough to feel a little loose, I guess."

"Ma'am, we've enjoyed your company but I think we must part now," Mark said. "Did you save out a tip?"

"No, boys, you got full value."

"Gentlemen, let us show our appreciation." They each came up with a quarter and put it on the table. The waitress gave them a smile and they headed out.

"The night has cooled off some. A wind off the sea, damp and salty. The boys are waking up some," David thought as they strolled along the street to the bus stop. Several groups of uniformed men – coasties, Marines, soldiers and a few Navy – were moving up and down the street. "Some of those guys are reeling," David thought. "Now one's aground," he thought as a Marine slithered to the sidewalk. David started over but the man's companions had him on his feet. "He'll be okay, looks like," David said.

Ben nodded. "If he was hurt, we should go over. But if his friends can manage him, better to mind our own business. They might think we was lookin' for trouble."

Half an hour later, they were settling down for the night. Two hours after that, the lights came on and some incoherent conversation woke David. "Pipe down!" someone called. "Oh, shorry," came the reply. A few minutes later there was the sound of vomiting in the head. "Oh, good grief," David thought. "I'm captain of the head this weekend. I should go see what happened.

"Oh, the dickens, whatever it is, it'll be there in the morning if I have to worry about it."

There were a couple of other loud entrances during the night, other sounds of vomiting in the head. "Well, four or five have puked in there," David thought to himself. "I bet at least one missed the john. But it would have been a waste of time to clean up before. It'll be there in the morning."

It was. "Almost stepped in it," David thought as he entered the head. "Nice clean floor last night. Yes, two sinks also. It could be a lot worse."

The dorm guard crashed the lids and men woke up in various states of grogginess and poor temper. "Seeing my first hangovers," David thought.

Two of his head detail men were among the hungover. "Oh, God, what a mess," Donald said. "Gangway!" He made it to one of the toilets and vomited.

"You going to be okay?" David asked.

"Dave was like a padre last night," Ben said. "Just coke and sandwiches."

"Oh, I get it. First time you've seen hangovers, huh?"

David blushed. "Well, yes, it is."

Donald managed a wan smile. "A hangover ain't nuthin', Dave. Headache, noise makes me jumpy, and then that whiff of barf got to me. I'll be okay."

"I hope you at least had fun," David said.

"Oh, yeah, I sang all kinds of songs and I impressed all the girls."

"Well, you left an impression, all right," said one of his friends. "I dunno if it was the impression you wanted, shipmate."

"We seem to have kept out of fisticuffs," Donald said.

"I'll say that for you, shipmate, you're a friendly drunk instead of a mean one."

"Let's get this all cleaned up before the rest of the guys comes in," David said. "Tracking it around will make things a lot worse. Especially if there are some other dicey stomachs."

They cleaned up the worst of the mess and then the morning rush set in. They were used to getting through their mornings in a hurry; fifteen minutes later, David's team was going about the routine cleaning behind twenty men.

Saturday night's rowdiness was somewhat the worse. David had spent the evening at the post recreation hall, drinking coke and shooting pool. There were several loud entrances and, around two in the morning, raised voices. David got up to find two men, buzzed or drunk, pushing each other.

"Guys, let's settle down. If the MPs show up, you'll both wind up on report and you'll be restricted to base for a month." The men did separate, looking daggers at each other and David but without coming to blows. David went back to bed.

"When I dismiss you, form up around the cargo net. You need to know what it's like getting into or out of the boats yourselves, so we're all going up and down a few times."

They looked down the side of the wall that simulated the deck of a ship. "Long way," one of the men whistled.

"About thirty feet," their instructor said. "Most ships' loading decks are twenty to thirty feet high.

"Keep your hands on the vertical ropes. Keep your eyes on the net rather than looking down. Take it real easy the first couple of times."

"First couple of times?" a voice asked.

"We're going to make the round trip all morning," the instructor said. "And give me twenty right now."

The coastie quickly did twenty pushups. "This is part of why we've done so much PT," David thought.

He was in the third relay. "It's a little easier if you're taller," he thought as he worked his way down alongside four others. "It feels wobbly, though."

A few minutes later he was working his way back up. "This feels a little more solid, but now gravity is working on us," he thought.

"Dear God, we're a sore bunch tonight," David thought in the barracks that night. He set up a chair near the head. "Anyone who wants, sit here for a massage after your shower," he said. He spent the next hour giving each of the men an amateur rubdown with some suntan oil. "God, please bless this coastie," he thought as each man sat. "Bless us all, please. Build us as a team, build each of us as Your son."

David was on the beach with half a dozen others. They were tailed onto heavy ropes from a Papa boat on the beach. "We've talked about broaching," their instructor said. "The coxswain is going to show you what broaching is like under easy conditions here."

As the Papa boat backed off the beach, the coxswain let the light wave action catch it and push it at an angle to its starboard. "Port side, heave," the instructor on the beach yelled. The tension on the line, on the same side as the boat was broaching but applied at the stern, pulled the stern around so that the boat was square to the beach. The coxswain let it go to its port and the starboard rope team straightened it out.

"How does this work during an operational landing with the enemy shooting at us?" one of the men asked.

"Well, it don't. If the beach is hot, you'll just has to get off by yourself. Once the beach cools off, you'll have beach parties to help you if you need it."

A few days later they were in the bay. David backed the Papa boat off of their favorite practice landing. About three lengths out, just turned around, the instructor said, "Smartly done, Ryerson. Now deal with this." He cut the engine off suddenly.

David barked – "I can really bark orders" – "Donald, wig-wag the rescue boat. Jim, get the messenger line out and bend it onto the tow line. William, make the tow line fast to the bollard. Look smart!"

In a few minutes they were under tow. "Takes skill to manage your boat under tow, just like under power," the instructor said. They towed for about half an hour, each man taking a turn as coxswain.

"Our turn to rescue," David said an hour later. Donald was coxswain. "There's the wig-wag and Tony is rigging the messenger line. Here it comes!"

"Beware fouling the prop or the rudder on the lines," their instructor yelled. They hauled in the messenger line and then the tow line, making it fast to their own bollard and taking up the slack. Each man took a turn as coxswain to tow, as they had taken turns being towed. "It's as sluggish as I expected," David thought.

A few days later they were herded aboard a transport with Papa boats on the deck. There were about a thousand Marines with them. The transport took them out of the bay, around the point and to the oceanside beaches.

"That sea is sure running higher than we've been used to," David thought as they moved out into the Atlantic.

The transport anchored about three miles from the shore. "Let's get the boats in the water," the chief called out. "Five of you and an instructor for each boat." Each section's instructor took over a boat and the coasties worked together to rig the hoists. They rode the boats into the water. "Quite a ride on the hoists. You can really feel the motion now."

Then they were handling the net and thirty Marines with gear were climbing down. "The boat and the ship are moving differently," David realized. "That's got to make it harder for the men to make it safely. Thank You, God, they're all aboard."

The instructor was coxswain for the first trip. "It's about the same as in the bay," he said, "but it's lumpier and getting off is harder." They drove in. David was acting as engineer; he had his hand on the brake that held the ramp as two other coasties removed the dogs. "Now, now," the instructor shouted as the bow grounded. David released the brake, the ramp slammed down, the Marines drove up the beach. "Barely got their feet wet," the coxswain said. "All right, get 'em back aboard."

The Marines came up the ramp and the coxswain yelled, "Retracting." He backed the Papa boat off the beach. "Ramp up!" he called; Donald helped David raise the ramp and two men set the dogs. "Coming around. This is when you're most likely to broach – try to be sure you've backed up enough, got some sea room." He turned the boat neatly and they made the run back to the transport.

The Marines climbed the cargo net and another group started down. "Baumberg, take the helm. Ryerson, you and Smith handle the ramp. Matthews, you can be engineer. Smith, you help him raise the ramp when we retract."

"Seven runs," David said to himself as they finally hoisted the boats aboard the transport. The ship raised its anchor and they headed back to the bay.

"Just a taste, boys," their instructor said. "We're scheduled to do this all week."

The next day was colder, grayer, windier. "This would be even harder if it were raining," David said.

Donald glared at him. "One more word about the day the Lord has made and you may have to swim back to shore," he said but he managed a wry grin.

The weather proved harder on their Army passengers than on the boat crews. "Well, we're busy and they're just going for a ride," David thought. "Lee side! Lee side!" was the frequent shout as men made room for their buddies to get to the side to puke. Some didn't get there in time. "My mop is in constant use," David thought. "Y'know, God, it seems a bit much to add this to my work in the head. It really does."

"What would it take to cancel practice?" one of the men grumbled near their instructor.

"A full gale, son. You got any idea what goes into a landing operation?"

"Just a little, bosun," the coastie said.

"Then you can figure that calling it off is a big deal. That's why you have to be ready to drive the boat in almost any conditions. Drive it safely, too. See that!"

One of the boats ahead of them had broached. "Let's get our men ashore and join the rescue boat." The student acting as coxswain was one of their best. They landed the men and retracted safely, then motored over to where the rescue boat was preparing to retrieve the broached Papa boat.

Shouts and wig-wags; it took both boats to retrieve the stranded boat. "There's a glum looking gang," David thought as they pulled the boat past the breaker line. The instructor was having some loud and obscene words with one of the men as he managed the boat. "I bet that poor soul was the coxswain. Looks like they're okay now." The rescued boat had restarted its engine and was under its own power.

"I am Gunnery Sergeant Thomas Walsh, USMC. You sailors should call me 'gunny' rather than 'sir' or 'sergeant', but I'd rather you used 'sergeant' or even 'sarge' instead of 'sir.' Again, the right handle is 'gunny.' I'll be your lead instructor for the chopped-down machine gun course.

"A machine gun is properly called a gun, so you should use that word for this training. The M-1 is a rifle and the 1911 is a pistol, but this is a gun."

"Gunny, we were told that a gun was too big to pick up," one of the students said.

"Go ahead, lift this one." The student went to the front of the room and hefted the Browning on its tripod. "Fair enough?"

"Yes, gunny," he said sheepishly and went to his seat.

"Being fair to my victim here, the term 'gun' is used just a little loosely. A shoulder-fired weapon that uses pistol ammunition, something like a Tommy, is called a 'gun' even though it's rifled. We've got a gun kind of like a Tommy called the Reising gun, uses the same ammo as a Tommy or a 1911. One man can work a Browning 1919 and even carry it, but it's meant to be a crew-served weapon, firing from a tripod, and that's why we call it a gun. It sure isn't a rifle or a pistol.

"All right, you've seen the movie. The most important and difficult element in using the Browning is leading. That's especially difficult and important in anti-aircraft operations. Bullets are fast but you have to learn to shoot where a moving target will be instead of shooting where it is. A running man, a boat or a truck, an aircraft. You're most likely to use the Browning against an aircraft or a small, fast boat. Even if you're shooting at a fixed target like a machine-gun next, your own boat or ship is going to be going like a bat out of hell."

Donald nudged David. "Ain't no Papa boat ever went like a bat out of hell," he said. David nodded and grinned.

"What's so funny, Ryerson?"

David blushed. "We were just thinking that no Papa boat ever went like a bat out of heck," he answered.

Gunny Walsh nodded. "Well, that's true enough, but there are a lot of other boats and ships. You and your buddy can give me twenty pushups for being smart-asses."

There were some grins as the two men came up front and did the punishment, then returned to their seats.

"We're going to have some lessons and some movies about learning to lead. In the end, you're going to have to learn when the time comes. Have any of you been bird-hunting?"

"Yes, gunny," said one of the men.

"Then you can vouch for what I'm saying."

The instructor showed them the key parts of the Browning – bolt, handle, trigger, belt feed, sights. "It'll fire 600 rounds a minute, except you can't fire it for a minute. There are different belts for different purposes, 50 to 200 rounds. If you hold the trigger, you'll go through 200 rounds in about 20 seconds and have to reload. Keep firing like that and the barrel will get awfully hot. We teach you to fire short bursts – conserve your ammo, get an idea of what effect you're having.

"The most important reason for short bursts is to avoid 'cook-offs.' Anyone know what I mean?"

A Marine raised his hand. "My father was a machine gunner twenty years ago, National Guard. He told me about it – the barrel was so hot it started firing on its own. They had to yank the belt out to stop it. Scared the shit out of everyone, Daddy said."

"That's a cook-off. And it scares the shit out of everyone. If you keep the barrel a little cooler by using short bursts, you'll make a cook-off a lot less likely.

"You'll have tracers, usually about every fifth round. The tracers help you see where you're shooting but..."

"They also show the enemy where you're firing from," Donald said.

"Yes. It's a dangerous tradeoff. Without the tracers, it's hard to figure out what you're doing. With tracers, the enemy has an aiming point. That applies more to dug-in positions; on a ship or a boat, the enemy will know where you are anyway."

The next day found them on the range with the machine guns themselves. "No grass growing under our feet," David thought. There were cans of ammunition at each station.

"Mostly you'll use the guns in teams, a gunner and an assistant to handle the ammunition feed. Sometimes the ammunition will be in a container on the side of the gun. Either way, that belt has to be kept feeding smoothly. Your lives depend on it and your buddies' lives depend on it."

The men were sorted into teams of two. "You, Ryerson and Baumberg, you were a good comedy team yesterday. Let's see you shoot as a team." David grinned wryly at Donald.

"We may have drawn a little too much attention," David said. Donald nodded. They loaded ammunition into the belts, from fifty to two hundred rounds in each. Every fifth round came from a can with rounds that had red tips. "Phosphorous – the tracer," the corporal handling their section told them.

Donald took his place behind the gun on its tripod. The corporal showed them how to chamber their first rounds – "You use the charging handle. It takes two cycles to get the gun in battery – has to do with the mechanisms that pull the cartridge from the belt and get the next one ready. Now, watch this close. Always, always run the charging handle with your palm up. If you get a cook-off, the charging handle is going to take off on you. If your hand is palm up, it'll just jump out of your hand, maybe scrape you a little. If you have your mitt wrapped around the handle, it's liable to yank your thumb right out of joint, maybe right off your hand."

David took his turn practicing the loading process. Then it was time to live-fire. Donald took his place again. "That target must be two hundred yards at least," he said.

David nodded. "Make sure of which target you're aiming at," he said. "It's easy to be one target left or right."

"That's for sure," Donald said. "I think I boosted my buddy's score by ten points back at boot camp."

David got the first belt, fifty rounds, ready. Donald, on command, opened the gun and put the belt in place. He closed the gun.

"Chamber your first round," the instructor ordered. Donald pulled hard on the charging handle and released it, then again.

"Short bursts. Fire when ready."

"The ear plugs are little enough against this noise," David thought as Donald fired and ten others did as well. "The line is just exploding. God help us all, what would combat be like?"

Donald walked the spurts of dirt into the target. David had the belt on the palms of his hands to help keep it running smoothly. "You're doing well with short bursts," David called to him over the noise and Donald nodded. The first firing lasted less than a minute before the cloth belt hung from the right side of the gun.

"Let them cool a moment before you open up," the instructor was saying. After a minute, Donald opened the gun and removed the last portion of the belt. David changed places with him and carefully loaded the next fifty-round belt.

David put his hand on the charging handle and the instructor slapped it. "Palm up, sailor," the corporal said. David changed his grip and ran the charging handle. "Twice," Donald said from his left. David ran the handle again.

"Wow, that's enough to fire a man up," he said as he fired his first burst. "The tripod is doing all the work. I'm close – just raise the muzzle a bit. A little right. That seems to be it. Keep control of the trigger. Short bursts." In about thirty seconds, his first turn was done also.

Late in the day, they were cleaning the gun. "That was a lot of bullets," Donald said.

"We were getting better as the day went on," David said. "I was a little scared that we'd get a cook-off at some point on the 200-round belt."

"I hope they let us shoot something like wood or even an old truck or something," Donald said.

"That'd be kind of fun," David said. But he thought, "Maybe too much fun. Destruction could be tempting."

"Dad? I'm at the train station. Yes, a little earlier than I thought."

"I'll be there in about fifteen minutes," Dad said. A porter took David's sea bag to the entrance and took a dime . "Glad you're home for Christmas, sailor."

The wind was cold. "At least it's just cold," David thought. "It'd be harsh, waiting in snowfall. The streetlights on the snow are beautiful, God."

The Buick pulled into the curb. Mom was hugging David before he knew it. "Let's get the gear into the back seat," Dad said. "Come sit between us, David. We both want all of you that we can get." They squeezed into the front seat.

They got home to find Marianne and Dan waiting. "I'll get your seabag," Dan said. He took the bag up to David's room.

"I'll be home about a week. I should hang up the stuff. It'll get creased enough in the future, I'm sure."

"It'll keep until tomorrow," Mom said. "We have some cake and hot chocolate. Down to the kitchen, everyone."

"Carry me down," Marianne said to David and put her arms up. She was already in her pajamas, up well past her bedtime.

"You're big for that, aren't you?" David asked.

"It's been months and months and you're bigger too," she said. He scooped her up and she put her arms around his neck.

In the kitchen, Mom put David at arm's length. "My first look in good light," she said. "Marianne is right. You're quite a bit bigger than when you left."

Dan stood back-to-back. "You're the same height but Mom's right. Your shoulders and your arms are bigger."

"So tan, too."

"I've been out in boats almost every day for two months," David laughed. "I bet I'm tanned."

"You look good, son. You went to write yourself man and you've made a real start," Dad said.

They all sat down in the kitchen. Mom ladled out cocoa and put cake on plates. "What's next for you, son?" she asked.

"I've got orders for the Samuel Chase. She's an attack transport ship with about thirty landing craft. I'm to join her in February. I'll go back to New River right after after Christmas. I have a ticket back for Sunday, the 27th. Camp Lejeune, it's called now."

"I think I saw that about Camp Lejeune in the newspaper – he was Commandant of the Marines in the Thirties and he died recently," Dad said.

"Yes, a big deal to the Marines. Anyway, I'll go back to North Carolina for several weeks. I don't know quite what they'll have me do. I hope I can help with training. That would be a lot better than three or four weeks of casual duty."

"Casual duty?" Mom asked.

"Means you're between assignments so you get every detail where a chief needs warm bodies. KP, barracks, weeds and seeds."

Dad snorted. "Weeds and seeds – taking care of the grounds?"

"Yes, dad. And there's always something to clean or paint or dust or move. Always potatoes to peel. Kind of a footnote to the first paragraph of writing myself man: he peeled a lot of potatoes. If you laid all the potatoes I've peeled end to end, the chief would bring out another bag."

Dad smiled. "KP. The bane of the junior enlisted ranks across the services. But it needs doing and it needs doing right."

"We had a company go down with dysentery at New River," David said. "I knew it was important because you had told me it was. That sure rubbed it in. We spent two days taking care of those men and their barracks."

"Did you pray for them?"

"I prayed for them and I prayed with them," David said. "Only a few wanted me to pray with them. And the boys started calling me 'padre.'" Dad smiled.

"You could be called worse," Mom said.

"Oh, I have been, Mom. The phrase 'swear like a sailor' comes from real life. Mostly the instructors at boot."

"I got called 'padre' the first time when I drank coke on liberty," David said. "Then after the company was sick, it kind of stuck."

Mom looked at him. "I'm glad to think that raising you with faith and compassion is sticking with you. You know a lot of the young men feel their oats and want to try living without their rules."

David laughed a moment. "I've cleaned up after a lot of them. Dad, when you told me to do what needed doing, you forgot to mention that could put me in the head a lot."

"In the head?" Marianne asked. She had been sitting on David's lap, her head resting on his shoulder and she seemed to be dozing at times.

"The head is what we call the bathroom," David told her. "It's a big room and a lot of men use it at the same time."

"That sounds nasty," Marianne said and wrinkled her face at him.

"It is, dear heart. But it's less nasty if people work together to take care of it and it's less nasty if someone in charge really tries to take care of it."

"It's still nasty," Marianne said and put her head down again.

David carried Marianne up to her room and plopped her on her bed. She crawled under her covers. "I know Mom will come in a minute and kiss you good night."

"You kiss me now," she said and put up her face. David kissed her cheek and went downstairs. Mom passed him coming up to tuck Marianne in.

Dan had other questions on his mind. "Did you like shooting?" he asked.

"Yes, I did. I shot expert with the rifle – the Garand. And I qualified with the .30 caliber Browning machine gun but it took a lot of ammunition to do it."

"Is the machine gun cool to shoot?" Dan asked eagerly.

"It's very exciting. When you're trying to walk it in, you track the dust and dirt you kick up until you hit the target. Or you use tracers. I'm worried about one thing – we talked a lot about leading targets but we didn't have any way to practice it."

"I never could lead a target," Dad said. "That's why we eat venison in season and not duck."

"Do the men really swear like the stories? You said they did."

"Oh, yes, they sure do. I get funny looks when I turn down beers and cigarettes and even more when I say 'dadgumit' or 'Sam Hill' or something."

"Some of the men might think you're being sanctimonious," Dad said.

"I'm sure you're right. But I pray over it and I ask myself about it. And I'm not. I'm just being myself – the boy you raised to a young man, hurried into a man's job and glad you raised me the way you did."

"Could you kill somebody?" Dan asked.

"That was a bull in a china shop," David thought. He paused and looked very squarely at Dan – not severely but earnestly. Dan seemed to wilt a little.

"I don't know, Dan," David answered. "I hope to keep out of that fix. If I'm on the gun and an enemy attacks the ship, I'll do what I can do. I think that would be easier than face-to-face. God spare me either one." For a change and a mercy, Dan seemed to be thinking that over instead of thinking up an answer.

They chatted a little longer. Then David said, "It's been a long day. You know what luxury I want most?"

"What?" Mom asked instantly. "If we can get it, it's yours."

"A real bath in hot water in a tub," David said and smiled. "Short, tepid showers for four months. I want a real bath. And sleeping in until I feel like getting up; even a day off in barracks isn't a day off."

Dad smiled. "I remember wanting a bath like that. Like after our hunting trips but ten times as much." David nodded and went upstairs. His parents heard the tub running a minute later.

"Gee whiz, I hope I don't want a bath the first night I'm home from a war," Dan said.

"I hope you get to live in peace because of what David and a couple of million other men are doing," Dad answered.

Saturday really was a day off. David was surprised to look at his watch and find that it was eight in the morning. He got up and shaved, then put on jeans and a sweater. He carried the uniform he'd worn on the train downstairs. Everyone was sitting quietly, waiting for him so Mom could start breakfast.

"Did we wake you up, dear?" she asked with a sharp glance at Dan.

"No, first time I've slept in since I left. Could I use the washer, please?" he asked. "Do we have any real plans today?" He put his uniform in to wash.

"Just to take it easy," Dad said. "I know you could use a couple of days of that."

Soon Mom was putting pancakes and bacon on the table, pouring coffee for the three of them. David tipped a little cream into his.

"I want to do a little Christmas shopping but I'll have to wear my uniform," David said. "I must wear uniform except at home or if I'm doing sports."

"Then we'll go into town this afternoon and shop," Mom said. "I'll be proud to show you off."

"Home," David thought, back in his room and looking at his books. "I've always heard that your house seems smaller if you've been away for a while and it does. I grew up in this room, in this house, but already I feel strange here." He heard the phone ring.

"David! Come on down. It's Andrea Matthews," his mother called.

"Hello, Andrea. This is a delightful surprise."

"I hope it gets better, David. Pastor Dan said I should ask you to ask me to go out. So will you take me to a movie tonight? Maybe 'Bambi.'"

"'Bambi?' Should I bring Marianne?"

"Just you and me. I conspired with your mother and you have the car tonight. We can have ice cream after the movie."

"I'd love that. Do you know when the movie is on?"

"Six o'clock. I'll see you at 5:30. But we have to do this correctly. Now that I've asked you to ask me out, you have to ask me out."

"Andrea, would you do me the honor of joining me for a movie and ice cream after? Say, about 5:30 tonight? Maybe we can see 'Bambi.'" Andrea laughed. "I'll see you then, Miss Matthews."

David looked at his mother. "Apparently I'm the object of a conspiracy," he said.

"Yes, well planned. How are you fixed for money, dear?"

"I've been earning forty dollars a month and I've been spending four," David said. "I brought some along so I'm fine, even with Christmas shopping. There's been so little to spend money on."

"No, Marianne, you'll have to stay home with Dan. We're going to be looking for presents for you two."

"Dave, will you take Dan and me shopping on Monday then? So we can shop for Mom and Dad."

"Sure, princess. That'll be fun too." David took a quick swipe at his shoes; they were already spit-shined. He put on his pea coat and his hat, then he went down the sidewalk with Mom and Dad. Their favorite stores were a few blocks away and it was better to save gas by walking.

"My, people are noticing you," Mom sad as they went into a department store. David blushed. "They think I'm a hero or at least a fighter and I'm still little more than a boot," he thought. He saw an Army officer exiting the store and he saluted smartly. Dad smiled to see it.

"A sweater for Marianne, a box of .22 ammunition for Dan," he thought. "Should I get something for Andrea?" he asked his mother. "It would be churlish to take her on a date tonight and miss Christmas in a few days."

"Well, Mom's giving me a look and I'm completely lost about what it means," David thought.

"You're right, but you should keep it small. It's a date, not a marriage proposal." They looked at jewelry and perfumes, but David's eye was caught by something.

"It's a little angel with 'This is the day' for a motto. Everyone could use something like this," David said.

"I think that's a good choice," Mom answered.

"People keep looking at me in my uniform," David thought as he held the door of the ice cream shop for Andrea. "Respect I have yet to earn, really meant for all the men at sea. The ones who have earned it." They took seats at the counter.

"I enjoyed the movie," David said. "Even if it's aimed at children. At least I didn't shoot Bambi's mother last year."

Andrea choked on her mouthful of ice cream, then managed to swallow it. "That was hardly a Disney kind of thought," she laughed. "I guess taking a hunter to see 'Bambi' could be like that."

"How is your school going?" David asked.

"I can take dictation at pretty good speed and I can type like a house afire," Andrea said. "How about your training?"

"I've written to you about most of it. We do the same things over and over – beach the boats, retract, beach the boats, retract. We take turns on the different jobs. Sometimes we go on the beach to handle broaching lines and move cargo around. There are a lot of jobs we might need to fill."

"And there are your other jobs. KP and stuff like that."

"And inspections – barracks, uniforms. We stand inspections in blues every Saturday morning."

"How often do you go into town?"

"We can have passes every other weekend, usually, but I've only gone into Jacksonville twice. Everything is less expensive on post and the big thing the men do off-post is drink liquor."

Andrea gave him a searching look. "I have a question I want to ask but it makes me squeamish," she said.

"It's just you and me and the chickens. You can ask."

"It's hard even just you and me and the chickens. David, do the men really...chase women a lot?"

David smiled wryly. "Oh, yes, a few of them do. Our chief calls it 'Russian roulette with your...' Well, you can guess with your what. Some of the women are just easy and some of them are harlots. Between being lonely and being, well, being men, I can understand. But I don't want in on it. Two of my friends have had...the clap."

"Are you very lonely, David?" Andrea asked.

"I would be lonely except I have family and I expect to come home. I think I'd be lonelier if I were going with girls who were strangers, girls for just a night. I do feel a little left out when the others talk about girls at home."

Their eyes met and they stopped talking. "We're both concentrating very hard on our straws," David thought. "I seem to have my foot kind of in my mouth."

"We need a different topic, I think. So, what about your cat?" Andrea said.

"Diablo is the least changed thing at the house," David said. "Although he has been all over me, more than last summer before I went off."

He took Andrea home a little while later. "Well, I can figure that out," he said as she put her cheek up toward him. He kissed her lightly and she went inside.

Andrea sat next to David at church the next day, her family in the row behind. "We are blessed to have Seaman Ryerson home for a few days," Pastor Dan said. After the service, many of his friends and acquaintances greeted him. "Some are conspicuous by their absence," he thought as one of the matrons was complimenting him on how he looked in his uniform. "Have a lot of the fellows joined up?" he asked her.

"My grandson left a week ago," she answered. "Yes, probably one or two boys a week have been leaving since you and Tim went in August. The draft board has been busy."

Andrea came over during the afternoon and they took Marianne for a walk. Again Andrea turned her cheek up and David kissed her lightly when they came to her house. "What's all that?" Marianne asked as they turned for home.

"I'm wondering that myself," David said.

"It's time to take us shopping," Dan said after school on Monday afternoon. "It's likely to snow tomorrow." David got his uniform on and his pea coat and they took the familiar walk to the stores. "I hope Mom will like this sweater," he said. "And Dad can use good socks any time."

"Socks and sweaters are great because you don't have to know the size too closely," Dan said.

David laughed. "Yes, that's why I picked them." Dan and Marianne were both a little short of money; David gave each of them a dollar to help out and they found presents for their parents.

"We can't really buy you clothes this year, can we?" Marianne said. "Because you just wear uniforms."

"Well, you'll have to get Mom and Dad to help you shop for me, or maybe Dan," David said. "I have very little space in the barracks and I'll have less on the ship when I get there, so you'll need to keep it small."

The package from Mom and Dad was oblong. David opened it: the logo said Western States Cutlery. "This is very nice," he said as he took the long-bladed knife from its handsome sheath. "We have knives, of course, but this one is a lot better than the issue knives."

"Take care of it," Dad said. "You're more likely to save your own life or someone else's life with a knife than with a rifle."

"I hope I've timed my visit well," David thought that afternoon as he went up Andrea's walk. She came out, put up her cheek for a kiss, and led him inside.

"David! Merry Christmas!" her father said.

"Is that a kind of searching look?" "And to you and Mrs. Matthews. And Jim."

He handed the wrapped package to Andrea. "And most of all to you, Andrea." She opened it and gushed a moment. Then she handed David an equally small package.

"I know how little room you'll have on the ship," she said. "But you'll find a place for this, I'm sure." It was also an angel figure, a tiny bit of white china.

"I'll call it my guardian angel. I'm sure a chaplain would sign off if necessary," David said. He held Andrea's hand in both of his for a moment.

Saturday evening, the day after Christmas. David and Andrea sat on the porch swing, wrapped up against the cold, clear night. "I enjoyed the movie, Andrea. I'm glad you asked me to ask you out again. Tomorrow I have to go back to work."

"I'm glad we could go out tonight," Andrea said. "You're going to be gone a long time."

"It could be a few months or a couple of years. The Marines have made a start in the Pacific and we are still waiting to start in Europe. The business in North Africa is just preliminary. I've been so glad to have your letters. Even your picture. But…" He was completely lost about how to say what was on his mind.

Andrea squeezed his hand. "You're afraid of tying me down. Or tying yourself down."

"Yes, I am. We're both young, at least as things were before the war. We weren't dating before I joined up. Now we've been to a couple of movies and gone on walks. It's been a great time but it's too little to say we're in love. Yet part of me says we're in love."

"David, you were awfully shy around girls in high school. You still are. Part of me thinks we're in love, too. But the war is in our way. I've got school and I'll be looking for a job in the summer. You go back to North Carolina tomorrow. You'll be working hard and living rough. We can't make promises now."

David looked somber. "Without the war, I'd probably be taking classes at the college. Working a part-time job. I'd be busy, maybe so busy I wouldn't have asked you out even yet. But at least I'd be in town. If I'd had the nerve to ask you out, we could go anytime. But this war is pushing everything back, who knows how far back. When I come home, I'll still need an education. I'll still need a job before I can think about marriage."

"Lots of people are making promises." Andrea looked a little sad. "They think they're making promises. I won't make you promises now and I won't take promises from you either. We have to just be fun for now."

"It's even a blessing," David said as he squeezed her hand. "In one way, I know I'm never coming home."

"What do you mean?"

"I was a fresh high school boy when I went to Manhattan Beach in August. I've been through boot camp and landing craft training. I've been shooting rifles and machine guns. I've learned to like people who are very different from everyone I've known. I've seen men drunk and heard them talk about things that are so different from what I've known or done. I've been living in a locker room instead of a home. I've been responsible for men's safety and I've had to rely on men for my own safety.

"I'm already different. David Ryerson from August is gone, just like the chief who signed me up said.

"And now...I'm going to see things that scare me. Things that I hope will make me stronger in God and stronger when I come home. But they will change me. The old soldier who has shell shock? The young man who has learned the ways of the world and who is still innocent? Could I be corrupted when I'm lonely and temptation comes on strong? I don't know who's coming home, but David Ryerson, December 1942, won't."

"You won't be corrupted as long as you think of your family and even of me. Or someone like me.

"David Ryerson, December 1942, has one more piece of fun you're going to give me before you go," Andrea said. "You're going to give me a real kiss and a real hug tonight. A man's hug and kiss for a woman. Not a Sunday school hug." He put his arms around her, felt her delightful body and her warmth. She took his mouth to hers and even got him to tangle tongues with her. "When I kiss you good-bye tomorrow, it'll just be quick on the lips," she said. "But I wanted both of us to have this. David?"

He was sitting silently, stunned. Finally he said, "I've been missing out on that?"

She smiled again, a little sadly again. "Yes, you have."

They went inside and he said good-bye to Andrea's parents. "Thanks for everything," he said as he shook her father's hand. Her mother took him in a hug and gave him a peck on the cheek. Andrea gave him that same wistful smile as she went to her room.

His parents seemed to notice something but they didn't pry. Marianne and Dan were already in bed. The adults had a last cup of tea and tried to talk. It was difficult. Mom was worried – worried to a state close to exhaustion.

David found an escape. "Could I ask one more indulgence, please? The thing I wanted most when I got home was a hot bath. May I take one more tonight? I think my next hot bath will be when I come home again."

Mom seemed relieved as she went up to start the tub for him. "I really do want a bath," he thought as he got ready. Soaking a few minutes later, he prayed. "God, please bring me safely home. To my family. To Andrea, maybe. I don't know Your will for Andrea and me."

He shaved in the morning. "I'm just as glad the train's early," he thought. "Might as well get going." Dan carried his seabag to the car after breakfast and they all piled in. Marianne sat on Andrea's lap.

"This is as awkward as I expected," David thought. Quick hug from Dad, a handshake with Dan. Longer hugs with Mom and Marianne.

The Andrea was in his arms. "A quick peck, just like she said," David thought. He entered the car and sat by a window, waving until the train pulled out. "A quick peck with a lasting impression."

"Seaman Ryerson..."

David faced aft and saluted the colors. "Sir, Seaman First Class Ryerson reporting aboard," David said as he saluted the officer of the deck. He presented his orders.

"All right, Ryerson. Messenger, take these three to their berthing section. Watch the route, coasties; the Chase is a rabbit warren until you learn your way around."

There were two other coasties in tow as they headed forward. Down a couple of ladders. Forward again. "Galley must be along here," one of the men said. "I can smell the cooking."

"You'll get used to it. Galley runs all the time when we're hauling troops around."

"Ma's cooking smells a lot better," the new crewmember said.

Down once more. "This is quite a large compartment," David thought. "Yet it feels cramped. Racks stacked five deep, lockers everywhere, just enough room to move between the racks."

"Here we go, Ryerson. You, O'Malley and Kramer will use these two racks. Lockers: Ryerson, Kramer, O'Malley."

"Top two racks. Lucky us," David said. "Where's the head?"

"Just forward. Get your stuff squared away. We're still overhauling, there are a zillion jobs to do and your work starts in about five minutes. Maybe ten."

David unloaded his sea bag and set up his locker as he had at Manhattan Beach. "We had a little more room at New River – Camp LeJeune, now," he thought. "But this is what we were getting ready for."

"This whole berthing space is really just a big locker room," O'Malley was saying. "Or a rat cage in a science laboratory."

"I'm David."

"Jack O'Malley." "Hank Kramer."

David went forward and looked at the head. "'Austere' would be a fair term," he said to his rack mates.

"So 'austere' means really small and it stinks and no privacy?"

David smiled. "Something like that. Also short, tepid showers."

"The place is already funky," Jack said.

"I imagine it's always a little damp, a little salty."

"Smells like a locker room in an old lady's attic," Hank said. David nodded; there was a mingled aroma of dirty clothes, mustiness and half-clean men's bodies.

"Laundry day is the only day it smells decent," one of the crew said. "I been aboard six months so I'm an old hand by Chase standards. Our section puts our laundry in on Mondays and we get clean sheets and clothes on Wednesdays. By Thursday we're back to this."

"All right, on deck with you." They followed a petty officer to the deck and he showed them an area of bulkhead that was spotted with rust. "I thought the Chase was a new ship," David said.

"She is. Only been in commission less than a year. All ships need painting almost all the time, though. And the area has to be thoroughly prepared." The petty officer handed each of them a rod like a crow bar and a mallet. "You're going to chip off the paint and rust and then another team will paint the area."

"How long have you been chipping on this ship?" David asked.

"Since the Navy bought her."

"How long do you think it will take?"

"Until the Navy sells her."

David dropped his chipping iron. "Dagnabit," he said. "Smack on my foot."

Jack guffawed. "'Dagnabit?' I'm sure you know stronger language than that."

"They want me to feel a little silly," David thought. "I've never caught the habit," he told them. "Never want to."

"Well, anyone but a padre would'a said 'shit'," Jack answered.

"And I thought I was done with that name," David said to himself. "I've been called a padre before," David answered. "I can live with that."

They knocked off at 16:00 and put their gear away. "That's a lot of scraping for only a little bit of metal," David said. "Tedious."

Jack laughed. "Probably this is just to keep us out of trouble."

David had his pen in hand a few evenings later. "We're still in port so I got your letter quickly. We'll get underway soon but I don't know quite when. If I knew, I couldn't say.

"We do a lot of cruddy jobs right now – fire watch when there's welding going on, KP by the hour, chipping for paint. There's always something to chip, something to paint, something to clean.

"The ship already seems crowded – the berthing compartment and all the working areas are compact, to say the least. The passengers' compartments are as stacked as our own berthing areas – officers' country being a little more comfortable. But only a little. The holds seem large and empty – they'll have to hold equipment, ammunition and food for a lot of men. We go into the holds very rarely.

"God be with you all, love,

"David"

"Everything in that should slide past the censors easily," he thought as he put the letter into its envelope and into the censors' bin.

Later, to Andrea, "I've been learning a game called ace-deucey. We play it on a backgammon board and it's kind of like backgammon, but it's quite different also. I'll show it to you when I'm home on my next leave. All my shipmates – well, a lot of them – play the game for small stakes. They give me looks because I'll only play for candy or points. But when money enters a game, even pennies, the game is very different. And some of the men will play for big money, whole paychecks.

"I miss you and my family. It's easier when we're busy – CPOs yell at us and keep us jumping. We'll be a lot busier when we're at sea. It's the evenings that drag. I've been to town with some of the boys. The USO does their best for us. Sometimes I'll go to a bar with the boys and I'll have coke while they have beers and we'll shoot some pool. After a couple of beers, I'm the best pool player in the party. I've got the nickname 'padre' again.

"God be with you in school. I love your letters.

"Your friend,

"David."

"Hey, David, you didn't say 'love'," one of the men noticed.

"As private as a goldfish bowl, this place," David said. "Andrea's a pretty girl and a nice girl. We're just writing letters."

"Then you're a fool," his shipmate said.

"Maybe I am."

They got underway a few days later. David looked at the convoy and the blimp overhead. "Anti-sub precautions," he thought. "The convoys are juicy targets for the U-boats. The blimps help keep them off of us."

"Yeah, those are good Joes," a crewman nearby said. "Everybody talks about the fighters and the bombers. The patrol guys – the men on the blimps and the ones in the PBYs – they get nothin'. They don't engage very often, but they keep the wolves away."

"How far will that one come out with us?" David asked.

"Usually about ten or fifteen hours. They fly long missions, those guys. Must get dull."

"Motion is starting separate the sheep and the goats," David thought a couple of hours later. "I just feel a little funny but some of the men are really green around the gills. I've already had to clean up behind a few who didn't make it to buckets."

Lookout duty was difficult. "Cold up here," he thought. "Wrapped as snug as we can be, but windy and cold and tossing us around some. Glad I seem to have gotten sea legs quickly. This'd be a bad place to be tossing cookies."

"Dear God, it's monotonous up here. Please help me stay alert. Hours of nothing up here but any moment we could be the difference between life and death. And it sure pitches more up here. I seem to be lucky about sea legs."

Another lookout took up a chant. "My breakfast went under the ocean, my luncheon went over the rail, my dinner is still in commotion, won't somebody bring me a pail?"

"Shaddup on lookout," the OOD yelled. "Sing out only if you see got something in sight."

"Killjoy," the singer mumbled. "If I do toss my cookies, I hope he's in the line of fire." Two cold, wet hours later, their reliefs came up and they went below to sleep for a few hours.

Two days later, David was chipping paint on deck when a shout went up from one of the masts. "Look out below, Mathers is coming down," someone was shouting. David went to the foot of the ladder as the man came down, blood streaming down his face. "Permission to take this man to sick bay," he called to the petty officer.

"Carry on, Ryerson."

There was a first aid kit nearby. David got a dressing onto Mathers' forehead. "What happened?"

"The stupid tub lurched and I hit my head on a spar," he said. "Lucky I had a good grip or I'd be overboard."

David went down the ladders before him. "In case you slip," he said. He helped Mathers down to sick bay where the corpsman took a look. "I'll get you sewn up," he said. "I dunno what it is. All you deckhands have scars somewhere between your eyebrows and your hairlines. Do you have to have a cut to get promoted to third class? Because you men will climb forty feet up a mast to hit your foreheads and get stitches."

David passed his hand over his own forehead. "I'll try to prove you wrong," he said to the corpsman.

"Oh, a few men escape," the corpsman said. "Nine out of ten have that scar, though."

Operation Husky

The ship anchored just south of Sicily. "July 10th, 1943. My first operation," David thought.

"Everything's ready, Allen," David said.

"Lower away."

A few moments later the motors ground and lowered the LCVP into the Mediterranean Sea. Their landing zone lay to the north. Allen engaged the propeller to get steerage. "Pitch dark. Hard to drive a boat in these conditions. God, be with us. Be with the soldiers we're carrying."

"If we gotta circle for an hour, at least the sea is pretty quiet," Allen said. "Let's get ready to load the boys." He pulled the Papa boat alongside Chase and a squad of soldiers joined the jeep that was lashed to the deck.

"Damn searchlights," Allen said.

"My first time among the dragons. Flashes. Explosions around those lights. Well, so much for them," David thought. "And the men who were working them. God, bring them to you, please. Give them grace, please, as I pray for grace for our own men."

"Get that jeep loose," Allen said as they lined up their approach. David and Mike began releasing the lashings that held the little truck in place. "Releasing a kraken," David thought. "God, be with us all. Be with all the men in this platoon." He saw a cartoon and a name on the hood of the jeep. "Give 'em Hell. Well, that's up to God, but give 'em all you have, yes. Our men need your help." David put his hand on the driver's helmet; the man turned to him, startled. "God be with you," he shouted over the rumbling engines of the jeep and the boat. The driver nodded.

"Landing stations," Allen called. David moved forward and undogged the ramp. The Papa boat hit the beach and the engineer released the brake to drop the ramp. The jeep scooted over the ramp and splashed onto the beach; the infantry squad ran with it and on up. Beside them, other landing craft were disgorging their loads.

A soldier lay on the deck. "I'll get to you as quick as I can," David shouted to him as the LCVP retracted. A few moments later the bow ramp was up and David dogged it. He scrambled to the where the man lay on his side.

"God, be with him," David whispered. "God is with you," he said to the injured soldier. He opened the catch on the wounded man's harness. Pulling Dad's knife from his sheath, he cut the shirt open, then cut away the undershirt. "Let's take care of this."

"This" was an abdominal wound. "A long furrow and then into his belly. I've seen some men with bad cuts and couple of men with broken arms or legs but this is the worst I've seen so far," David said to himself. "God be with us," he said aloud; it was all the time he could spare for a conscious prayer.

"Mark! Get his wound kit!" Mark was already opening it. "This could have hit the man's spine. Let's get a better look. Buddy, can you feel your feet?"

"Sailor, I've got so much gear on I hardly know I've got feet."

"I'll check that in a minute. Let's get the sulfa on and put on a dressing." They shook out the life-saving powder and applied a dressing to the entrance wound. "That's only bleeding a little, soldier," Mark said.

"We need to check for an exit wound but we have to be careful about his back," David said. The three crew except Allen were gathered around the wounded man. "We'll turn him in a minute but let me do this first." David cut the laces and took off the soldier's boot. "Okay, soldier, can you feel my hand??"

"No. Oh, God, am I paralyzed?"

"What can I tell him? I think he is but sometimes theses things get better. Sometimes they stay this way." Out loud: "I hope it's going to be all right, buddy. Try to push your foot against my hand – just your foot. Keep your body still." The soldier's foot remained still.

"Oh, God, it hurts." Mark was cutting the soldier's sleeve to give him morphine.

Someone had brought the Stokes stretcher and laid a blanket inside it. Two men were cutting the soldier's harness and getting his gear out of the way. "Did someone clear that rifle?"

"Yes, cleared and secured."

"Keep him lying like he is as much as you can," David said. "We'll have to get him into the stretcher and we'll check for an exit wound while we do that. The Stokes is pretty good at keeping his back lined up; we just have to be careful getting him into it." Silently, "Thank You, God, that the sea is pretty calm. A rough sea would make this even worse."

"Everyone got a good grip? Roll left a little." They eased the soldier to the left and David inspected his back. "No exit wound." That could be either good news or bad; at any rate they didn't need to get a dressing onto his back. "Keep a little strain on him head to foot. Stretcher here. It's more like put it on him than put him in it. Okay, ease the stretcher down. Cinch him in. We've done what we can for him. Buddy, I'm David. What's your name?"

"Carlton Oakes. I'm from Santa Ana. California. Can I have a drink?"

"Carlton, I'm sorry, nothing down your throat. It'll tear you up inside." David dampened Carlton's lips with a little water on his fingers. "A kind of baptism," he thought.

"Smoke?" Mark asked and offered a pack. Carlton nodded. Mark put the cigarette to Carlton's lips and lit it. He and David knelt by the stretcher and secured it. Carlton puffed; Mark took the cigarette every little while and tapped off the ashes. "I've seen 'em so bad I had to light the cigarette in my own mouth and give it to them," he said.

"Now that's a real Samaritan," David thought.

They were alongside the Chase. "One wounded!"

"Already?"

"He got shot before he could get ashore," Allen said.

"Block and tackle, stretcher party," the bosun on deck called. In a few moments they had rigged the hoist on the stretcher. "Carlton Oakes, of Santa Ana, California, God be with you," David prayed.

Allen was inspecting the Papa boat. "We're only making the usual amount of water and the holes in the side are well above the waterline," he was telling the bosun in charge of repairs. "We can make another run immediately if we need to. As long as we can ride a little high."

"We do need you right now," the disembarkation officer said. "Let's get the next load on board." Two jeeps with cases of ammunition were lowered into the cargo deck; about a dozen soldiers scrambled down the nets. Two minutes later they were headed back to Gela.

"The sounds are a lot louder. Shells, machine guns. Too loud to make out the small arms fire," David thought as they headed ran up onto the beach. The engineer dropped the ramp. "God be with you," David thought as the jeeps and the squad headed up the beach and into the storm.

He saw several small groups moving their way. "Hold the ramp!" he yelled and waved his arms at the engineer. Three groups ran aboard with litters. They set them on the deck. One of the litter bearers was wearing a bandage himself but he returned to the beach with the others. Not a word had been spoken.

One of the men had both legs heavily bandaged and was a little groggy. "We all got patched on the beach," he said, somewhat thickly. "I think everyone got morphine.

"Did you get sulfa pills?" David asked. "I think we have some if you didn't." Orders were to use a casualty's sulfa pills rather than one's own but he would be able to replenish easily.

"Yeah, I did. Hard on my gut. Can I have a drink, please?"

"Get hit in the belly?"

"No, stepped on a mine. Thank God everything is from my thighs on down. My balls are okay."

David smiled. He helped the soldier to drink from a canteen. "Glad to hear it. What's your name?"

"Gleason, Tom Gleason."

"I'm David." He scrambled over to the coxswain. "Allen? I'll stay with the wounded. Hang onto their stretchers, help them if they need something."

Allen nodded. "Go ahead."

The hour-long ride back to the Chase was actually dull. The wounded men subsided into morphine-induced hazes. As they approached the ship, Allen said, "Ryerson, go ahead and announce us."

David went to the side and called up, "Three wounded on litters."

"We'll hoist you up to unload," the bosun called down. The crew quickly rigged the hoisting lines and motors rumbled. When the boat was level with the deck, David and Creole lifted the first litter to the litter team on deck, then the second and third. Allen was working on refueling. "Let's get these crates on board," the bosun said. David helped wrangle pallets of ammunition and rations. "Hard to say which is more important," he said to one of the deck hands.

"Yeah, but if I were on that beach, I'd be more worried about ammo than food. They can scrounge for food and I bet they will."

"It'll be hard on the villagers if they do."

"They'll give them some money. But yeah, it'll be hard on them. This whole invasion is going to be hard on them."

"Are we invading them or liberating them?"

"Some of them wonder too, I bet. I guess it depends on how much you liked Mussolini. But I bet they're all fed up with the Germans."

The runs to the beach began to blur. "We've been up since last night," David thought. "We're maybe a little punch-drunk. We're turning around faster each time. Except for the wounded. Every trip, more wounded. God, be with them all. God, help me do what I can for them." Since he was almost cargo once the Papa boat backed off of the beach, Allen was leaving him to help the wounded. "I'm getting too used to this," he thought as he moved among the litters with a canteen and a pack of Creole's cigarettes. "The groans. The blood and the bandages. Knowing what's under them. God, spare me from becoming jaded by this. Please, God, help me with fortitude but keep me compassionate."

The boat crews and the deck crews could unload the wounded more safely and quickly by hoisting the boats to deck level. As soon as the injured were off the boat, men and supplies and equipment loaded up. "Glad I got to the head last time," David thought. "And I'm sure glad someone thought to get sandwiches to us. Who knows when we'll have time for mess call?"

Allen looked at him as they loaded for the next run. "You're doing good work with the wounded, Dave. Why are you a deck man instead of a corpsman?"

"I wonder about that myself sometimes," David answered. "Somebody at Manhattan Beach thought I'd be good with boats, I guess. And the Coast Guard needs more of us than corpsmen."

"He'da made a good padre, too," Mike said. "He's the only man in our berthing section who drinks coke on liberty. Leaves women alone, too."

"It's getting dark and this will be our last run today," Allen said. "We've been on watch almost twenty-four hours. We've got to knock off for at least a while, clean up and get some sleep or we're going to get clumsy and hurt someone."

Two hours later they were securing the boat on its cradle. "It takes us a couple of hours from when you say 'secure the boat until we actually knock off," David said with a rueful grin.

"Gotta have the boat ready at all times," Allen said. "You know that."

"Yes, I do," he answered as he secured the water cans in their locker. His shipmates had checked all the lines and Allen had refueled the diesel tanks.

"It took another hour before I got in here," David thought as he soaped up in the shower. "God, I should remember that I'm blessed. All of my shipmates are safe. I'm getting a shower and I have a rack. The men ashore have got little more than dirt. At least we got plenty of food and ammunition to them. God, be with the men ashore and especially be with the men in sick bay. The doctors and the corpsmen are still at it – saving lives, sometimes helping the men have easy deaths. Gather them all, God. Even the enemy." He had seen some wounded with German uniforms. "Whatever repenting they need, please help them do it. Whatever grace they need, please grant it to them." David pulled the handle. "A meager ration of water to rinse off. Even that poor excuse for a mattress is going to feel like a feather bed tonight." He lay down and tried to pray again but he was asleep before he knew it himself.

Operation Avalanche

"The new guys are shaping up well enough," Allen said. "I hope so. I'm expecting to hand this boat over to you and to go teach the new crews after this operation."

David looked up from the instruments. "Am I ready to be a coxswain?"

"You're as ready as I was. More ready, I'd say. You've had almost a year under my tutelage. You've done one operation under me and here's our second. I was coxswain on my first operation in North Africa – learning the way a cat learns how to swim. Two real operations and hundreds of practices – that's a lot more than we started with in North Africa."

They circled for another thirty minutes, then came alongside and got the net in place. Their platoon came down the net, thirty-six men and their equipment. A lieutenant was in command. He went among the men as best he could on the crowded deck; Phil and George also checked the men. "Lifebelts all around. Safeties on. Check your buddy and your buddy checks you."

Ahead lay the beach at Salerno. "High tide and dawn. An hour's run and the soldiers are having a rough time of it."

"Lee side! If you're going to puke, lee side! Your left, dammit!" Phil was trying to manage the seasick men and it was going poorly; the deck was pitchy enough and now there were slicks of vomit as well. David shook his head. "Phil can try to herd the guys but they're packed too tight to do much," he thought. "God, be with them. God, settle the sea a bit, please. Help these men get on the beach ready to fight." He checked his instruments; everything was running smoothly. "God, thank You again for the engine and all the people who made it run so well. Thank You that my job is still delivery and pick-up. Please bring our boat and our crew safely through today."

The parade of wounded began on the second run. "When did you start smoking, padre?" Phil asked as David produced a pack of cigarettes and a lighter.

"Oh, nope, not me. I got a carton from the gee-dunk shop for the wounded. Seems to help them almost as much as the morphine, if they're used to smoking. Mark taught me that at Galeta."

"Damn coffin nails are expensive," Phil said.

"Cost less than the blood of these men," David said. "I haven't had to light one in my own mouth, like Mark sometimes has."

David knelt next to a man with bandages on his chest and abdomen. He was breathing heavily. "The Lord is my shepherd," David began and realized the man wasn't breathing at all. His eyes had become glassy and fixed. "Mark, take a look with me. Is this man dead?"

Mark leaned over to listen for breathing, rested a hand lightly on the man's chest. He put his ear to the bandage on the man's chest and it came up with a streak of blood on it. "Yes, padre. Your first?"

David stroked the dead man's forehead. "My first. I've brought in wounded but they've all made it to the ship before this. I know some of them died later."

"We'll wind up taking him back, or someone will. We can't keep the dead on the Chase. Graves Registration will get him to a temporary grave later."

"The grave will be temporary. The loss is forever," David thought. He went to the next man, helped him with a little water. "Smoke?"

"No, thanks."

David smiled. "Me neither." He continued his rounds, not seeing how his shipmates eyed him.

One of the wounded was talking with Mark. "When did the landing craft get chaplains?" he asked and nodded toward David as he draped the dead man with a tarp.

"Chaplain? Oh, padre. He's just like that. He's the engineer. You'll see him checking the engine every couple of minutes. Prays over every wounded man. I think he prays over everything, really."

"You sent for me, Bosun?" David said as he entered the warrant bosun's office.

"Yes, Ryerson. We've been reviewing some of the men who may make good officers. Do you think you want a commission? It would probably a reserve commission, only for the length of the war, but some shavetails are going to become regulars. And Officers' Country is a lot more commodious than your berthing section."

"I've given some thought to asking, sir, but I don't think I'm a good candidate for officer. I sure don't plan to make the Coast Guard my career. And I'm glad you think I show potential, but I don't believe in myself doing well as an officer. Too young, too...well, sir, too soft as many would reckon it. I doubt I could keep a section in hand as well as I manage a crew."

The bosun nodded. "I can understand that. You may well get a larger craft some time, but I agree that you're outstanding where you are. I think you'd make a better officer than maybe you think you would, but only someone who really wants the bars should go to OCS.

"Dismissed – and with my respect, Ryerson."

"Back to the Chase tomorrow and who knows what's next?"

"The invasion, David?" Dad asked.

"Mine not to reason why, Dad. We all know it's coming but I'd have to keep my mouth shut if I did know anything."

"Yours but to do and die," Mom said. "To do and die."

"It's a risk, Mom. I'm a lot safer than the infantry are."

"The Chase is a juicy target for any Kraut U-boat," Dan said.

David looked at him sharply. "Mom knows that, but she'd be better off without hearing again," he thought. Dan seemed to catch his thought. "But you'll be in a convoy and the Kraut won't have a chance."

"We call her the Lucky Chase. We've been shot at and bombed at but the Germans have always missed us. If a sub has ever made an approach, it broke off before it could attack. The Germans have got very little to come after us except the subs and the subs have been on the losing end for months now.

"Even the boats have been lucky. We've had holes in them but the crews have all come in safe."

Mom looked at him intently. "David, have you seen men die?"

"Yes, Mom. I've seen men die. I've prayed over them during their last breaths. Just a few, thanks be to God."

The discussion got harder; Mom was more distressed by the minute. Finally Dad said, "Tomorrow is coming early. Let's go to bed."

"My last night in this bed for who knows how long? Each last night, it's been longer until the next trip home. God, oh God, be with Mom and Dad. Dan and Marianne think I'm bulletproof. Mom and Dad know better.

"And Andrea. We're still telling each other it's just fun, but it's more than that. And she knows I'm not bulletproof."

The boat crews were chatting in the auditorium. "This is it," was on everyone's lips. "Checkin' everybody's name on a list – first time I've seen that." There were covered boards at the front of the room.

A Navy lieutenant rapped on a lectern. "At EASE," he said loudly. All the men in the room fell silent.

"This is the most secret possible briefing you will ever attend. You thought we were serious about security before? This is the most serious we're ever going to be. If you let anything slip about this, you'll spend a very long time in prison if you're lucky. If you're not, you'll spend a very short time in prison. Follow me?"

The men looked around soberly. "This will be it," David thought. "We know we're going to go into France. Now we find out how."

An aide removed the first board's cover. The map was large enough that David could make it out even though he was fairly far back in the room. There was a chorus of whistles and grunts.

"That ain't Calais," Mike said.

The lieutenant was speaking. "This is the Calvados-Cotentin coast of Normandy, due south of us. The Germans have put a lot of concrete and a lot of firepower along the whole coast but they have focused on the Pas de Calais. They figure we're coming by the shortest route and to a big port. Calais is the most obvious and logical place to invade. We've been helping them think that with some Hollywood song and dance around Dover.

"We figure they'll need at least twenty-four hours to decide the operation in Calvados is the real thing. Maybe longer. The longer they sit, the better for our men going ashore – and for you also. If they give us twenty-four hours, they'll give us Europe.

"You'll get the day and the time when you sail and it'll take some hours to get where you're going. But you need to know your landing areas. We'll cover the broad plan now – as much as you need to know about the broad plan, anyway. You'll get more detail on your beaches in later sessions."

The lieutenant began pointing out areas on the map. "There are going to be five landing zones. From east to west, they will be Sword, Juno, Gold, Omaha and Utah.

"The Brits will be going in at Sword and Gold. The Canucks are taking Juno. We've got Omaha and Utah. You can see that Utah is actually farther from Omaha than the other landing zones are from each other. Utah spills over onto the Cotentin peninsula.

"There are going to be paratroops inland to tie down the Germans and help establish the link-ups. And that's all you need to know about the airborne operation.

"How many of you have made a landing before?"

"About a dozen of us," David thought as he raised his hand.

"This one is going to be different. H-Hour will be at low tide."

"Sir?" David raised his hand again.

"Yes, bosun's mate."

"May I ask why we're going in at low tide, sir? We've always gone in at high tide so the beach would get bigger instead of smaller."

"I don't have the whole story for you, bosun. Two reasons I know about. First, the Krauts have learned to expect us at high tide and we figure they won't be looking for us on a low tide. Second, they've been damn busy on those beaches, building obstacles and mining them. If the first wave goes in at high tide, you're liable to get your asses blown sky high. It could happen anyway."

David and his crew looked at each other. "Well, that's a new way to do it," David said. "God, be with us all. We're going to need You," he said to himself.

The briefing continued. "All of you will be assigned training areas that are as much like the beaches you're going into as we can find. That means that even saying what your training area is like would give the Krauts some ideas about where you're coming. Most of all, it'll tell the Krauts that Calais is not the invasion zone. God only knows how many men could get killed if they figure that out.

"The Krauts can read maps as well as we can. They know where we can get ashore. They can't beef up everything from Dunkirk to Biscayne. They've been putting their best units and their heaviest equipment around Calais. They're putting a lot of second-tier units into the Calvados region. Lots of old men, lots of kids, lots of men dragooned from other countries. But stay realistic, boys. The fortifications and equipment in the Calvados region are still plenty tough. Old men and young kids can kill you just as dead as the Panzer Lehr can."

"The who?" Mike whispered to David.

"Their elite tanks. They're no threat to the ships offshore but they could play hob with us on the beach if they're close enough."

"We've got to get past the beach obstacles before we worry much about tanks," Phil said.

"We just have to miss the obstacles. If the tanks are near the beach areas, they can shell us like any artillery. Worse because they're mobile."

A few days later, they were at their next briefing. There were ten crews. "You will take no notes at these briefings, nor will you discuss them in any other location. You will have charts when you need them. You men are going to be embarking Big Red One soldiers for Omaha Beach. This section is going to go in at Easy Red." They gathered around the chart. "Pilot boat to the east and here are your assignments, line abreast."

"We're in the second wave, two over from the pilot," David noted to himself. They pored over charts and aerial photographs. There were even a few photos taken from surface level and looking at the beach. "Some tough guys in mini subs, I guess," Phil said.

"These summer houses will make good landmarks."

"If they're there. The Krauts may demolish them or our shelling might. Real estate along the shore in Normandy is a bad investment right now – sell short if you own any. So make sure you've got the natural features too. Those bluffs will be there even after the old ladies have done their worst."

"Any of the bombardment falls short, it's going to play hell with the landings," another coxswain said.

"Yeah, but that's someone else's problem," their briefer said. "Anyway, the fleet will lift the bombardment a couple of minutes before the first boats hit the beach. We're not going to shell our own guys."

"Sufficient unto the boat is the trouble thereof," David said.

"Huh?" Mike said.

"We'll have plenty to do, plenty to think about," David said.

"Your job is to get your men and equipment ashore and get out," the briefer said. "There's going to be a boat only a few minutes behind you. You're only a couple of minutes behind the first wave, so I'll be surprised if anyone is trying to get on your boats. If someone manages to get aboard before you raise your ramp, maybe get some wounded guys aboard, okay. But you're there to deliver. Don't wait for anyone to get aboard. Get off that beach and get back here for more men and more stuff. Keeping ammunition and food and fuel moving to the beach is going to be just as important as getting the men and equipment ashore.

"We'll tell you when to start bringing wounded back, and there's going to be a lot of wounded to bring back. God only knows how bad it's going to be. The brass are saying it'll be fairly easy – the bombardment is supposed to dig foxholes, the resistance is supposed to be weak."

"Sir, I've heard that before. In Italian. You'll understand my doubts," another coxswain said.

"Officially, I'm supposed to reinforce the optimistic line. But yeah, bosun, your doubts have a lot of company."

They spent the next hour going over assignments, positions in the assault group and landmarks. "Make sure you know what's east of your landing zone and what's west of it," the officer said. "We've run this play before and you may well be east or west of your intended zone."

"Leeway, sir."

"Leeway, smoke, losing the pilot boat, being shot at – all of those things can louse up navigation, even more when it's the first time you've seen the place."

"We're getting better," Phil said. "We can launch with no lights on. The soldiers are getting pretty good with the nets."

"The rougher the practice weather, the better. We have to learn to help the soldiers aboard when the boat and the Chase are moving out of synch."

"So we do this over and over," Mike said. "Onto the beach. Disembark. Then back to the bus and do it all again."

"And again and again and again," David said. "Whenever the real thing comes up, every run up and down the nets and every trip to the beach means one less soldier drowned. One less soldier who slams into the deck and gets knocked out before he can fight."

"They'd be lucky if they all broke their legs trying to board. Then they'd be out of it."

David shook his head. "The road home lies through Berlin. The road to Berlin starts at Calvados. That's a terrible truth, but it is the truth."

"Well, better the Papa boat than infantry," George said. "We just have to get off the beach and back to the ship. Those poor sumzabitches…"

"They're going to have to kill a lot of men," David said. "Those poor souls."

The word filtered through the Chase with astounding speed.

"Did you hear about last night?"

"God, what a cluster…"

"Was it really that bad?"

"I heard five ships were sunk. God knows how many men."

"Scuttlebutt," David said. "A near miss and now it's a disaster."

"Was a lot more than a near miss."

Finally their section chief called the group together. There were similar meetings all over the ship.

"This is classified, men. You say anything about this, you're going to prison or you're gonna get shot. The Utah Beach taffy got mauled by some German torpedo boats. Couple LSTs were sunk and a bunch of soldiers and sailors are dead. I don't have the exact numbers. My orders are to tell you men not to even talk about it among yourselves. Hell, I know better than that. But don't say nothin' in letters and don't say nothin' where anyone can hear. Anyone."

David sat silently. "God, please gather all those souls to you. Please be with their families. Some of them were married. Some of them were probably fathers. All of them were sons. God, be with all those who lost men who are dear to them."

David and his crew hooked onto the hoists. "Raise away!" he called. Motors ground and the Papa boat rose to the deck. "Let's put her to bed," he said. The crane team set Lucky 13 on her cradle and they spent the next hour making sure she was ready to go.

"How many runs did we make today?" George asked.

"I think it was seven. You think we're tired? Those doughboys have been up and down the nets all day. Running ashore, running on the sand. Our job is tough but theirs is tougher."

"Yeah, I'd a lot rather drive the bus than ride it."

"We gotta get this invasion underway soon." David heard some form of this a hundred times a day. "Restricted to post. Three weeks now. Beer's gotta be running low."

"Hey, padre, how is this restriction affecting you?" The jibe came from one of the men David knew less than some others.

"It's sharpened my acey-deucey game. The best players have had to stay aboard and I've learned a lot from them. If we're socked in another week, I'll be champeen of the whole ship."

"Are you good enough that you'll put money on the game now?"

"Gaming for money is a losing proposition, shipmate. If I get behind on candy, I can let it go. If I were behind on money, I'd think I had to get it back somehow. Besides, I've never been a lucky fellow. I won't bet on the sun coming up in the east – not money, anyway." "Seen too many paychecks wiped out that way," he said to himself. "They all know the risks of gambling, they'll just be miffed if I say anything about it. And the boredom is getting to everyone, me as much as anyone else. The bosuns are down to busy work to try to keep us out of trouble – have to keep projects small because we might get under way any hour."

"Well, I think I know the invasion plan now," George said as he surveyed the vast armada. "We'll sail ahead of all these other ships. Then the ships will form a line and the soldiers will just walk from Portland to Calvados from deck to deck and we'll take them in the last half-mile in the Papa boats."

David laughed. "Looks like we could do that," he said. "God," he breathed, "thousands of souls. Billions of dollars that could have done Your other work. You alone know how much blood is going to spill. You alone know how many years of joy and achievement and sorrow will be lost. Be with us all, dear God. Be with us all."

Throughout the day, smaller craft brought infantry and equipment to embark. All of the men and equipment had their places in the vast holds. All of the men and gear had their narrow intervals. Lucky 13 had its own narrow intervals to prepare and to load, to drive into the beach and then return for more men and more equipment. "Paper pushers," George was muttering.

"Paper pushers are winning the war," David said. "Well, they're making it possible to win the war. Try to get all of this stuff and all of these men ready without plans and lists and orders."

"I guess you're right, but still. Paper pushers. Carbon-copy commandos."

"And here's our carbon copy," David said as one of the men handed him a schedule. "Mimeographed. Mimeo Marauders? Less pithy than your carbon-copy commandos."

June 6...1944

David went over his own gear. "Canteen. Some D rations. Dad's knife. Helmet. Life jacket." He looked over his men; all of them were ready.

"Food and water in the lockers, skipper," George reported. "Fire extinguishers. All emergency equipment checked." David nodded. The tension was familiar from the landings at Sicily and Salerno. "God, You were with me then. Please be with us all now."

"Lower away," David called. The davits squealed and the motors grunted. Lucky 13 settled into the water and they unhooked the lowering gear. David moved Lucky 13 into the circle of landing craft.

"First wave is lined up. We'll circle while they get loaded and head out. We're slotted about five minutes behind them. H-hour plus five." Phil, Mike and George nodded. They knew the plan.

The dark was less than absolute but all artificial lights were out. Shadows were enough, though, shadows and the sounds of other boats. After an hour of cautious circling in the dark, David kicked Lucky 13 into the next slot in line. Papa Boat 12 began to load its soldiers.

The first wave was moving south toward the beach. Phil stood beside David. "That'll be a hell of a show there," he said.

"Hell is right," David answered. He knew that Phil and he saw that word quite differently. He caught Phil's startled glance. "Padre, that's the first time I've heard you use that word."

"First time I've meant it," David answered. "If you can do your time in Hell while you're living, that's where it'll happen." "Phil," he thought, "you're a fine fellow but we'd have a hard time figuring expiation and salvation very well. And we're busy."

David looked up at the cargo net over the side of the transport. Men were starting down, pressed by the ranks above them. Mike and George were in the well to receive their own load of soldiers in a few minutes. "That's a load they've got," he thought. Every man was bulky with helmet, rifle and pack, gas mask – Intel was scared about nerve gas – ammunition. The men had enough personal gear to be campers on a three-day trip along with their fighting gear. "They've been crowded and seasick for three days, they've hardly slept. I'm surprised they can hang onto the nets at all," David said to himself. "If the air could turn blue, that language would do it," he said to Phil. Some of the climbing men hesitated but they were pushed by men above them on the nets. David could see the coxswain in 12 tweaking the boat to hold position, his bowman and sternman handling the net and waiting as the soldiers began to transfer to the boat.

One of the soldiers fell from the very top of the cargo net. There was a scurrying of heads visible above the gunwale of the Higgins. "Just get him to the back of the well and keep loading. He can ride the boat back," David heard someone shout. "He's a lucky cuss," another voice said. "Good time to bust your leg, soldier."

David had his doubts. "He'll be all right if Boat 12 is. But if that Papa boat takes a hit, he's going to be in a bad fix. And the ride in and out is going to be rough anyway if he's got a broken leg."

The men in Papa 12 were handling the net, getting it out of the well so they could move ahead. The coxswain moved the boat out and forward and David sidled up. Between the deck crew and his own men, they got the net ready in a minute and the soldiers started down the nets. David used an easy skill to keep the boat as close to the Chase as he could without damaging contact, only glancing touches of the fenders and occasionally metal on metal. He snickered to himself each time the hulls clanged and the soldiers would jump.

Soon the well deck was crowded and the men were wrestling the cargo net out of the way. All of the soldiers were aboard safely. Noise from Lucky 13's engine, noise from the Chase's deck motors, noise from the decks. Shapes of men, ships, boats – everything was vague, still a couple of hours before dawn. All conversation was hollering. "Mike! George!" he yelled. "Check every man's life belt." David started away; the next boat was already moving into position. The clockwork was creaky but it was insistent.

A soldier with a holstered .45 – obviously the officer - was standing with Mike. They were talking with a soldier wearing corporal's stripes. He had his life belt over his shoulder. "Get that around your waist, Carlson," the older soldier said.

"Damn thing'll be in my way."

"You got a mother still, son?" The "son" was a laugh, David thought. The older soldier was apparently in his mid-20s, but the corporal did look to be only eighteen or so.

"Well, yeah."

"Do it for her, Carlson. There are a lot of ways you can get killed today and drowning would be stupid. You know from the practice runs; we're going to hit the water hard and heavy. That belt will keep your head up until you get your feet planted."

Mike chimed in, "Drowning on the way in would be stupid. If you fall off my boat with a life belt, maybe you'll float long enough for a pick-up boat to pull you out. No belt and you'll sink like a rock."

The corporal nodded finally. The officer yelled, "Everybody check your buddy. Check your life belts." David had pulled Lucky 13 from the side of the Chase and moved into the circle of boats forming for the run in. A few minutes later, Lucky 13 passed a bobbing figure in the water. "That's why we have lifebelts," David said to himself. He saw that the officer had seen the bobbing man. The officer pointed with his arm and David shook his head. "Dear God, let a rescue boat find that man. He'll be hard to find in the dark. It's got to be a rescue boat; too many of us, lanes too tight and I could get more people hurt if I try to get to him."

The orders were clear: even rescue boats would have to work in the dark. A glimmer at sea now would give the Germans an hour's warning, an hour that would cost many men their lives if the Germans got it. The lives of hundreds on the beach weighed more heavily than the life of one man in the water.

The last boat of their section pulled away from the troop ship and the section formed line abreast. "12 on my left, 16 on my right, we're on our way," he said to himself. "God, be with my hand today. Let my every act be a prayer, please. Let my eye be sure and my hand be strong to put these men ashore in safety and ready to fight. God, be with every man on this boat. Please." Trying to keep in formation, he headed straight for the beach that he knew as Omaha, Easy Red. It would be an hour or more before they grounded. The sky lightened as they went, the high-latitude June sunrise masked behind the clouds. "It's like indirect lighting in a fancy office." Mike and George were scuttling along the hull to their gun tubs at the stern.

The rough Channel was having its predictable effect. "The port side is the lee side! Port! Left, you dogfaces! If you're gonna puke, try to puke over the left side!" Phil was shouting. The boat was riding low and the men were crowded. "Phil's wasting his breath," David thought. "They're kinda stuck. Too crowded to move to the side. It's going to stink pretty bad." The well of the deck was already spotted heavily with vomit and more came up every few minutes. "Well, they'll be wrung out pretty soon."

There was cursing all over the deck. Over the cursing, David heard consternation. "We're shipping a lot of water," the officer said to David over the din.

"We've only got a little freeboard," David answered. "A little water and we could swamp. Phil, get the men bailing," David said. "They may have to use their helmets. Anything we have."

Phil grinned at David. "Miserable ride we're giving these guys. They may decide the Germans are less of a problem than this boat is."

A cold, dark, miserable hour later the shore was visible and soon they were lined up for the last sprint to the beach. "If you call ten knots a sprint. Well, for Lucky 13 it is."

Now the sounds from the beach had become far too clear. Nearly constant waves of explosions. Some noises from engines. A chattery sound. "Machine guns. Just like Galeta and Salerno but a lot more of it.

"Second wave but that's going to be just as bad as first wave. They've been getting ready for two years. And their spotters had to have seen us at first light. Well, knowing about us for an hour is better than if they'd known yesterday." He saw that a number of Papa boats were already wrecked on the beach or just offshore and he was afraid. "God, be near me today. Be near me, God, and be near every one of us.

"Well! I'm just chanting it over and over. God, be near us. God, be near us. I'm just trying to be right with You. You know my heart better than I do.

"God, if I lose the boat, please help me put the boys on the beach first.

"Where the dickens are we?" Tracking with the pilot boat, seeing what he thought was their intended grounding area, he realized that they were well to the east of where he thought they should be. "I can find the Chase all right when I get turned around. It'll be the Army's problem to figure out where their men are." He got the captain's attention. "Sir, we're east of where we expected to be. I don't know how that will affect you and your men joining up with other elements," he shouted over the noise.

"Me neither, sailor, but at least I know about it," the captain shouted back.

"Mike! George!" he said. "Grounding stations!" The two men left the gun tubs; they had not fired a shot. Mike moved to the bow and undogged the ramp; George moved beside Phil to help with raising the ramp when they got off. Phil was leaning on the brake handle that kept the ramp in place.

The surf was demanding his attention now. The landing was only a moment away. The boat went hard onto the sand. Phil released the brake on the ramp winch. The ramp slammed into the water. "Get 'em off! Get 'em off!" David yelled.

There was really no need for his men to get the soldiers off – their officer had maneuvered to the front and was leading them at an awkward run. "Charging or fleeing? Thank You, God. The boys are only knee-deep. We're right up on the sand and it looks like they've got good footing." Bullets were zipping into the deck but they were passing through the well and missing all of the soldiers. The deck was empty.

"Wait, one man in the well. He's been hit. We'll just take him back." "Mike! Get ready to dog the ramp! We'll take care of that guy after we get turned around!" "God, be with Him and help us get him back to the Chase," he managed to pray.

Phil and George were starting to raise the ramp; Mike was waiting to set the dogs. "Retracting!" David hollered. He reversed the propeller. "Gotta take it easy here," he said to himself. "Focus on that house on the beach. Keep it straight while I'm backing." After a moment of hesitation, Lucky 13 pulled away, got its face off the sand and become fully a boat again. "The ramp is up and dogged; we're far enough back not to broach, and we're ready to come around and head back to the Chase. Mike is coming back to check the man in the well."

The shell struck. There was so much noise that the shell's shriek was drowned out and the explosion took David by complete surprise. The blast threw him into the air and he barely had time to realize that Lucky 13 was kindling and junk beneath his feet. He hit the water head first and his helmet fell off. The impact stunned him and the cold water squeezed his chest like a huge fist. Another hand spun him and then pulled him up to the surface.

David's head broke the surface and he gasped his lungs as full as he could. He was halfway on his back; the full lifejacket was designed to keep him positioned with his face above the water even if he couldn't swim. Splats in the water; zipping noises past him. "Bullets! I ought to be scared. Why am I calm? Too much to be scared of." He tried to duck under the water. His life jacket was keeping him at the surface.

"Wow, and I thought the soldiers had it hard. Which way is up? Which way is the beach? There!" Now that he had his feet under him and the water was only chest-high, he could ditch the life jacket. "Need to get my head down. Some gunner might see me enough to aim and there are so many bullets anyway. A bullet hits the water, it loses most of its power in a few feet."

"Cold! My fingers can barely move. Gotta get these buckles off. There, now the last one." As soon as he pulled the jacket off, his feet touched bottom again and he looked around. "Where's my belt? Fell off somehow. Canteen gone, food gone. Oh, shoot, Dad's knife is gone. 'Your God knows you have need of these things,'" David took a deep breath, submerged and felt around. "Well, the belt's gone. So is my helmet. Got to get ashore. Maybe I can get onto another boat. Maybe I can find the guys."

His life jacket bobbed away among the hundreds he could see near him. He felt like he'd abandoned a friend. Life jackets, heads that were moving or only bobbing, debris. Patches of red in the water. "God be with them. God be with them all.

"Where are the guys? Those are my guys. Where are they? They all got tossed around, sure. They may be close if they're alive." He shouted as loudly as he could: "Phil! George! Mike! Lucky 13!" "Well, that's a waste of time and breath. I'll see what I can do when I get to the beach." He looked around; the bobbing mass of debris and bodies and thrashing men was just too confused to see if his men were there. The zipping bullets made him feel very visible. "God, help them. I don't see how I can help them right now." David might have been angry, he might have been sad, he might have been worried. Fear had washed over every other feeling.

David crouched as low as he could, holding his breath and keeping only his eyes and forehead up as he looked around. His clothes were too heavy to swim and the water was really too shallow; instead, he waded and used his arms to help him along. Every few moments he had to lift his head so he could breathe.

The waves were threatening to push him off his feet and the intense machine gun fire was sure to find him if he remained exposed. Mortars were dropping into the water as well. "God, bring the guys in if they're alive. Gather their souls if they're lost." After a moment, he added, "Please. But I've got to look after myself now. Please, help me get through.

"Gotta breathe." He lifted his head just enough to gasp in, closed his mouth, and ducked down again. He found himself swallowing some salt water. "Much of that and I'll start puking." There – one of the beach obstacles, its legs rising out of the water. There was a shape on the end of the pole. "Teller mine, sure as shooting. Dangerous place but it's the only thing that looks like cover."

"Down, boy, the lower the better." As he moved forward, pushed around by the incoming waves, he had trouble keeping his footing and keeping up his duck-walk posture. Every few seconds, he raised his head enough to take a couple of deep breaths. The splashes and zips played around him all the time and each one seemed to know where he was – except that they all missed him. The fear of the machine gun fire faded a little; his brain was overloaded and the bullets were so many that they lost some of their power to terrify him. "Wore that part out.

"More Papa boats coming in. They're getting men ashore. But they're pulling back too fast for me to catch one."

As David moved forward, forced more and more into a crouch to keep his head low, his feet tangled in something more than beach sand. "The water would be about to my waist if I stood up straight." He kept in his crouch. "It's big and it's squashy. I know what it is. There's a guy right in front of me, dead under the water. He's gotta be dead or he'd have come up for air." Leaning forward into the water, David groped with his hands a moment and he knew he was right. There was a body across his feet. "You have to be an American."

David wanted to just step over the corpse; the man was past all help, after all. "All help but God's," David said to himself, as much of a prayer as he could muster that moment.

His last evening at home came to his mind clearly. Mom had looked terrible. "I'm scared of a lot of things, David. You could get killed. You could get crippled and spend your life on crutches or in a wheelchair. You could...you could just disappear and we'd be asking God where you are for the rest of our lives." "You got a mom, buddy? A wife? A dad? Maybe a sweetheart. They need to know. It'll be better than wondering."

Kneeling in the water up to his chin, David heaved the weight to the surface. The face was gone but the dog tags were still around the neck. David found that he could bring one knee up and support the weight on his raised thigh. "Okay, soldier. Were you on my boat? Maybe, but you were probably first wave. Two tags," he said. "Leave the main chain behind so you'll have a name if someone finds you. I'm gonna take the small tag because, I'm sorry, but you're probably going to wash out to sea. Looks like the Channel will be your grave, buddy. Even if the tide is coming in, you may wash back out. Lotta ways you could get lost on this beach." David took the beaded chain from the man's neck. He detached the smaller chain and got it into a pocket. "That could wash off your neck," he said. He passed the longer chain through a buttonhole, struggling in the cold water with cold hands, making a lark's head knot. "If someone finds you, you'll have a name," he said and let go of the body. It remained below the low waves. "Your family will get the news either way. They will if I can get through. I hope they will."

David moved forward again. A few yards later his duck-walk left a lot of him above the water. "I'm going to have to break for it now," he thought. Kneeling in the water, he checked his orientation on the post he had seen. There was barbed wire around the object, which was a long pole with one end on the sand and two legs at the end toward the water. "One of the beach obstacles you wanted me to hit, eh, Rommel? Well, you blew up my boat instead." David ran as fast as he could toward the obstacle. He could see some men were lying near it; living men, for they were moving around. Some at least were living; other forms lay motionless. A few were writhing.

David was running as fast as he could but his run was awkward. The sudden immersion, the cold water, had made his muscles and nerves stiff and he ran in a jerky gait up the beach. The sand was soft enough to slow him also. The spits of sand near him, the continuing zing of ricochets, got him moving faster than he knew he could. In a few seconds he was sprawled with the other men in the limited shelter the obstacle offered.

"Damn it, sailor, what are you doing here?" said a soldier with staff sergeant stripes. "This is our show."

"Ran into a problem with my boat," David answered. "It disappeared right after I went flying out of it."

"Lot of that going around. How are the boys you brought in?"

"I had just pulled off and they were on the beach. I was just trying to get sea room to turn and head back for the next wave. They were all okay when I pulled off – or at least they had got off only knee-deep and they were running like crazy up the beach. Things are confused after that. I had three men with me. I should try to find them. Four men – there was a man down on the deck."

The sergeant shook his head. "They're on their own for now, sailor. If you go running up and down the beach, you're going to last maybe a minute. All you can do is stick with us and hope for the best. Maybe you'll get out of this alive."

David nodded. He had been afraid to try to find his men and he was glad for a valid reason to focus on surviving himself.

A soldier with a corporal's stripes had rolled over toward David. "I bet things got confused. Did you know you were bleeding?" The man touched the side of David's head and it suddenly stung.

David whistled. "News to me, buddy. How bad does it look?"

"You've got a gash a couple inches long. If you hit it on a car you'd think it was big but it's pretty small for a shrapnel wound. Still bleeding some. It's running down the side of your neck and behind your ear. Lot of it been washed off as you came in, I expect. You got a first-aid kit on you?"

"It was on my belt with my other gear and I lost the belt somehow. I've got precious little on me." David felt around. "Lost my helmet when the boat got blown up and I was flipped off it." The corporal got out a package with a compress and helped David tie it over the gash on his head. Their movements were clumsy because they had to work while lying prone.

"I think we missed the sulfa powder," Tim said.

"You said it was shallow and I pretty much soaked it in salt water so it should be all right. Thanks for helping me," David said.

Joining Big Red One

"You may be wearing dungarees but you just joined the Big Red One, sailor." The corporal turned a moment and David saw his unit patch. "Your old job has been overcome by events, as you might say."

"What am I going to use for gear?"

"Supply is irregular just now," the sergeant said. "Just what I needed, jokers," David said to himself. "But requisitioning is pretty casual now also." The sergeant pointed to a form on the beach a couple of yards away. "We'll try to cover you while you go draw yourself some gear."

David scrabbled across the sand. He was lying beside a dead soldier now. He took off the helmet and found himself looking at the face of a man about his own age. The skull had been shattered. David put the helmet on his own head and realized that the dead man's blood was oozing down his neck. He wrestled the ammo belt from the waist of the corpse and buckled it around his own waist. Finally he took the Garand from the dead man's limp hand. "Thanks, buddy," he whispered. "God has you now and I need this more than you do." David thought about the body he'd left under the water. "Let me get one of your tags," he muttered. "This shelling is liable to bury you or blow you apart or the tide may wash you out." Again he took the tag on the short chain and looped the longer chain through a button hole. "It may still come off but this is the best I can do. Your mother? Your wife? Your sister? Someone will need to know." David put the tag with the other one in his pocket. "God, it's terrible to be making a collection of these," he prayed a moment. "But I'm liable to have a bunch of these before we're done."

David scrabbled back to the group huddled by the obstacle.

"We're gonna have to haul ass outa here pretty fast," the sergeant was saying. "There's a mine on this obstacle and the Krauts are shooting the mines off. They have all the prime places pre-sighted for their mortar teams, too. And that machine gun fire is bound to get us if we stay. Sailor, what's your name?"

"Ryerson, David P. Bosun's mate third. Coast Guard. Maybe I should stay here, try to help casualties or something."

"We'll just call you sailor." David winced inwardly. "Well," he said to himself, "the right word is 'Coastie' but this is hardly the time." "You'd better stick with us. You'll get killed for sure if you stay here. How much do you know about the M1?"

"I've shot the rifle on the range, all of the landing force have."

"Moore, you and sailor check out that rifle. I'm going to scout for a place for us to go."

Tim rolled beside David. "Okay, before we try to go inland, let's check that rifle. See what shape the action is in. Here's the safety – on, off."

"I know the basics," David said. He wiped the loose sand from the action and he pulled back the charging handle. The breech seemed to be clear of sand. "There may be sand in the barrel," he said to the sergeant. "There's a round in the chamber."

"There's a rubber over the barrel, see? To keep water and sand out," the sergeant said.

"Yes, sir, but the condom's torn apart."

"Call me 'sarge', sailor, I work for a living. I'm gonna have you take a test shot somewhere there are only Krauts." The sergeant pointed toward some bushes well up the beach. "That way looks clear. Put the rifle on this support and keep your face away from the breach. We'll know in a second if the barrel's jammed."

David released the safety. He pulled the rifle into his shoulder and turned his face and body away. "This is an awkward way to hold the rifle but I want my face away if that bolt blows up. Here I am, squeezing softly as if that would matter. God, if I must do this, please let this weapon work." The rifle fired normally, hardly audible among the thousands of rounds that were firing all around. "The noise is incredible; everything is shooting or exploding." The beach was a cacophony of small arms firing, mortar rounds and mines exploding, the ripping sound of the advanced German machine guns. He could barely hear the sergeant giving orders.

"Well, the barrel's clear. You're armed now, just like a dogface," the sergeant said. "You sailors are sometimes pretty careless with rifles. Couple of things I want you to keep real close in your mind today. First, that rifle is your best friend on this beach. Second, you need to keep the bore clear so keep the muzzle up when you hit the dirt. You're gonna hit a lot of dirt today. Last thing, you keep your safety on until you have the muzzle pointing somewhere. It's awfully easy to fire the thing when you're running around." David nodded. "I know all this," he thought to himself. "Army has a dim view of us coasties as soldiers. But this is a good time to keep my head down and my mouth shut."

"I'm Tim, David," the corporal said. There were two other men getting ready to move and David heard the names Bob and Jason but he missed who was which.

"Okay, Emily Post is happy. If you want to cheat the undertakers, listen up. You see that group by the wall to the east?"

"Yes, sarge," they answered.

"Grouping like that is a bad idea. Learned that in Sicily. A group like that will draw machine-gun or mortar fire like sugar draws flies. When we move out in a second, we're going to that clump of bushes over there. Keep some separation. Two by two if you want but only two and keep some distance between pairs." A moment later the sergeant's words were borne out; a mortar shell blasted near the clump of men he'd pointed toward. It was too far for David to see what the result was.

David was asking himself, "How long has this been?" He'd been scheduled to ground at 0635 but he knew the timing had been thrown off. "It feels like an hour since the boat blew up and it feels like three minutes."

The sergeant was saying something else. "Some of the Krauts may be trying to sight instead of just spraying. Here's how you do it. Jump up, run like hell, and drop. You're up, he sees you, you're down. Every time you drop, count four to ten Mississippis, but a different count every time. Then do it again. It'll take five or ten sprints. Remember, keep spread out as you run and keep spread out when we get to those bushes. Keep me in sight as much as you can, but try not to look right at me or a sniper will figure it out and shoot my sorry ass."

David was still trying to sort out how to keep an eye on the sergeant while not looking right at him when the order came. "Move out! Move out!"

"You're up! He sees you! You're down!" David had made perhaps five yards as he dove into the dry sand. His face scraped like a really bad shave. A few rounds threw sand around him, one onto him. He counted four and took off again. He sprawled into the sand. "God, be with us. The only time we're in more danger than when we're running is when we're lying still. God, be with us.

"Muzzle up, muzzle up," David said to himself as he dove into the sand. "Be a lot easier to keep the barrel clear than it will be to clear it. And if I start shooting, I'll forget to check the barrel, sure as little green apples."

"You're up, he sees you, you're down," he chanted and dove into the sand again. The soldier he thought was named Jason was a few yards to his left.

"Shingle now instead of sand. Easier to run on. Four Mississippis – up and run."

This was the last lunge to the limited shelter where the sergeant had ordered them to form up again. He dove into the pebbles and he heard Tim land beside him with a grunt. "Mother fucker, not again."

"Tim, are you all right?"

"No, God damn it. Just a nick but I can't reach it."

David rolled over and looked. There was blood on Tim's back, on his shoulder, and the uniform was torn open. Tim gave David a pack from his ammunition belt. David examined the wound a minute. "That should get stitches," he said. "It's almost like a knife did it."

"Yeah, a graze. Got one on the other shoulder too. We were too busy to ever get stitches in it but it healed up okay."

"It's pretty shallow but it's about six inches long."

"Put the sulfa on it and help me wrap it up, will ya?" David shook the antibiotic powder across the gash and held the field dressing in place. It covered most of the wound at least. They managed to tie the bandage in place around his chest. "God, heal Tim, please," he said silently. "The red badge of courage," David said out loud.

"Yeah, I read that."

David laughed a moment. "Well, teach me a lesson," he said. "You understand, you speak kind of roughly and I was quick to think you didn't read much."

"I don't but I graduated from high school. Wrote a report on that book."

David smiled at him. "And now you've lived it out."

"Yep, I been among the dragons. You?"

David nodded. "But not like this. This is my third operation but my boat got through the others all right. I should try to get back to a boat, get back to the ship."

The sergeant heard him. "Fat chance, sailor. I dunno when we'll have enough control of the beach to try to send wounded back to the ships. If you try to get out there now, you're just going to get killed."

Tim snorted. "Look around you, sailor. You're in the Big Red One now. Gonna be quite a day for you."

"The sarge is right. God, I'm here now and I'll have to manage. God, be with us all. And please remember me if I forget about You today." The noise was still overwhelming.

The sergeant was still talking. "You were skipper on your boat but you're my problem now. Stick with Moore there, listen good, and we'll try to get through this."

Another group of four men joined them. David thought maybe they were getting too bunched up and might draw a mortar round or other fire after he'd seen the other group hit. But one of the men in this group turned out to be an officer. "Two bars, an Army captain. A Coastie captain is a lot higher up." The captain and the sergeant were conferring. The captain had apparently taken command of the group, now totaling nine men.

"Easy Red is about the middle of the beach. Now we've been pushed pretty far to the east. The Krauts are putting most of their attention toward the center of the beach, where most of the men are. We've got a chance of working our way around further east, getting up this bluff that's sheltering us a little, and maybe surprising the Krauts. Come at 'em while they're looking somewhere else."

"This sound is…amazing. So loud it's just amazing instead of scary. What's that shriek coming through all the noise?" A large explosion shook the top of the bluff some distance away – David could only guess how far, something like half a mile, it seemed. "Navy's trying to do something, anyway," the captain said. More shells followed. David glanced out to sea. "Those destroyers are awfully close in. They could run aground if there's a shoal. Oh, God, help them!" One of the destroyers had vanished behind an explosion. "It's going down fast. Please, God, get the men off and to safety."

The captain was speaking. "Now look. Staying here is a sure way to get killed. We have to get up this bluff. It's the best way we can fight and, funny thing, it's the safest thing we can do right now."

"Cap'n, are you sure about that?"

"Hell, no, corporal, but I'm sure we'll get killed if we stay put. Better to die fighting for a chance to live than lying flat. So that's what we're going to do. Let's move out." The captain spotted David. "Navy, who the hell are you?"

"Coast Guard, Ryerson, David J., bosun's mate third class, sir."

"Coast Guard, eh?"

"We're just calling him 'sailor', cap'n," the sergeant said.

"Have you buddied up?" Tim put his hand on David's shoulder. "Well, sailor, you stick with your buddy toward the back of the patrol. Abel, take the point." A corporal moved to the front.

"What am I doing here?" David asked himself. "I'm a coastie. I belong on a boat with the next wave. But it looks like it will be hours before I can try to get back to the Chase. The firing across the beach is too heavy. The Papas are getting in and out much too fast to load anyone from the beach. 'Get your boat off the beach and get back to the ship.'" Those had been his own orders and they would remain the orders that the other coxswains would follow for some time. "Besides, the sergeant and the captain outrank me. I have to obey their orders. My own best chance to survive is with this squad. But I still want out of it. God, be with us."

His duty was clear. Tim gestured for him to go ahead as Tim took up the rearguard.

"You're up. He sees you. You're down. You're up. He sees you. You're down. Once more!" Bullets continued to patter around them but they were less intense than a few minutes before. They came to a barbed-wire barrier. "Gotta blow that," the sergeant said. "Anyone got some Bangalore tubes?"

Three of the men did. They crawled forward and pushed the first tube under the wire, attached the second tube and pushed it forward, attached the third tube. One of the men attached a wire to the blasting cap at the end. They scrambled back and connected the wire to a detonation switch. "Fire in the hole!" the man with the switch yelled. "Fire in the hole!" He twisted the switch and there was a heavy blast. "What the hell? That was louder than three tubes."

David raised his head. The wire had been separated and a large crater had also appeared. "Had mines under the wire," the sergeant said. "Figures." The team moved through slowly, the first man probing with his bayonet. If there had been other mines, they had apparently blown up with the Bangalore tubes. "He's probing awfully fast but we have to keep moving," Dave thought.

The bluff was steep and its surface was very rough. That was their salvation; there were a lot of places for their hands and feet. The soldier on point was apparently a dab hand at this; he was finding a route and the others were following in turn. It was slow going and David's going was the slowest; these men had trained for this kind of terrain and he was having to figure it out as he went. Two things besides the climb were starting to register in David's mind: "I'm thirsty and I've got to take a leak soon. That's awfully banal. This hardly seems the time or place."

David needed all his breath to climb anyway. He was carrying less than the infantrymen around him, a Garand and some ammunition and one canteen. The others had their packs with ammunition, rations, even a change of clothing. David still found the going called on all his strength as he tried to keep up with the patrol.

Clouds of smoke began to roll across them. "Hard to breathe," David said to himself.

"There's a favor," one of the soldiers was saying. "Some of the shelling has started fires in the brush. I thought it would be too wet to burn."

"Good thing it's wet," another soldier said. "That smoke will make us hard to target." They continued climbing. The smoke brought tears to David's eyes and burned his nose, his mouth and his throat. He tried to figure out a mask but nothing in his clothing or gear would serve. He would have to get through it like the others. "God, be with us," he managed to breath.

They continued to climb. For some reason the Germans seemed to all be somewhere else. There were sounds of mortar rounds passing overhead toward the beach. Each time the rounds passed over, the captain watched and seemed to listen. "He wants to know where they are," David said to himself. "Is he planning to dodge them or go after them? I'll know pretty soon, I guess."

"Here's a path," the man on point called. "A made path, cap'n."

"It probably leads to the German positions, then. We'll see if we can use it."

"What's that sound?" Dave turned his head to the right; he saw some men. The helmets were the wrong shape and he could see they were moving into firing positions. "Those are the enemy." The cut for the trail made both a screen and a bulwark. "Perfect shooting position." David brought the rifle to his shoulder and put the front sight on the German in front. "That guy has some braid, so he's probably the officer. If I stop him, it'll goof up the squad. That black cross on his chest is a perfect sighting point." David fired.

"Wow," David said. The brass cartridge popped off of David's face as the German fell. Suddenly the two squads were engaging and rifle fire crackled. A second German went down and clutched his leg. The other Germans grabbed the men who were down and began trying to withdraw. David left them to it. "God be with me if I killed him. God be with them."

Tim fired at the fleeing Germans and swore when they dropped out of sight. "No fair play, sailor. If they get away, they're going to try to kill us. Next time, keep trying."

"They're just guys like us."

"Sure, guys like us. But they have their orders. If they get the chance, they're going to sight on you and kill you. Or me or Jason or someone who's got a kid at home. Damn Hitler sent them and maybe it ain't their fault, but that's what they're gonna do. Not your fault either. Blame Hitler and his buddies. Blame 'em when we're done."

"He's right. My duty is to this squad," Dave realized.

Tim was still talking. "I been in Italy. Maybe they're just guys like us but some aren't. I saw some God-awful stuff in Italy. War is hell and all that, sure, but I saw some stuff. You read about it in Stars and Stripes too."

"Maybe they didn't do anything like that."

"I got no idea. But it doesn't matter. You and me, we got our work to do. We got to stop all the Krauts we can. I've seen Krauts were wounded and still shooting, even shot guys who stopped to try to help them."

The squad moved along the trail. There was a ripping sound up ahead. "Machine gun position," Tim said.

"We'll have to clear it out," the captain said. "Everybody seems a little dubious about that," Dave thought as he looked around.

They were on the right side of the position – a relatively small concrete bunker but it looked impervious. There were some shell holes nearby and marks on the concrete. "They've probably been shook up by the Navy," Tim told Dave. "The Krauts call this a Widerstand. Pillbox. They got 'em all over."

The machine-gun crew seemed to be focused and firing to the front and to the left. "They don't have a clue we're over here," David thought. "What's the captain going to have us do? God, bring us through this, please.

"But someone has to die here. Us or the Germans. God, whoever dies, be with us all."

The sergeant and the captain had conferred. "As soon as we start shooting into that embrasure, they're going to turn that gun on us. We have to make ourselves small and we have to make a volley into that embrasure count. We need every rifle, sailor, so you too. Wilson, I want you ready with a grenade."

"I'd be awful lucky to put a grenade in that from here."

"It's worth a try. If you miss the embrasure, it'll put their heads down and it'll give us a chance to run up and put a couple of grenades in from close up. I'm open to other ideas if you got one real quick." No one offered anything.

Dave lay next to Tim as they took up positions. He could see the embrasure but that was all, except for the barrel of the machine gun out the front. Its muzzle flash showed even in the sunlight.

The sergeant had taken a place in the middle of the group. "Ready, fire!" he yelled. The volley was ragged but rapid. David couldn't tell if his own shots were entering the embrasure or not. There were plenty of dust puffs from misses. "Pings – I just made one. The magazines are out. Reload fast." He was just closing his bolt when the soldier with his grenade let it fly. It hit just above the embrasure and burst. David clicked his safety on.

The men in the squad ran forward and three of them dropped grenades into the Widerstand. They all ran to the side and got clear of the embrasure as the grenades began to go off. Three loud explosions, one prolonged scream, silence. "Dear God, what happened in there?"

The entrance to the Widerstand was ajar. One of the soldiers pushed it open with the muzzle of his Garand and yelled "Kamerad!" There was only silence. He pushed the door fully open and went in crouched. A moment later he gestured the others in.

"That's worse than I expected." David could barely hold his gorge. A couple of the men were cursing and one did vomit. There were two dead men on the floor. "And on the walls. Even on the ceiling. We did this?

"What part of this did I do? No way to know. God, be with all of us – the dead and the killers. The dead were killers too."

The captain examined the machine gun. "MG42. Damn good gun but this one needs to be destroyed. Anyone know how to disassemble this?" One of the soldiers raised his hand. "Take it apart and bring a crucial part with us. Firing pin, maybe. You can have it for a souvenir."

"It's still hot from shootin' our boys, but I can handle it," the soldier answered. A few moments later he put the firing pin into his pocket. He scattered the other parts of the firing mechanism around the floor. Another man, the biggest in the patrol, slammed the muzzle into the concrete floor four or five times and managed to bend it. "That's one gun out of action."

"All right, let's move out. This was good work."

They formed up again. Tim and David were at the back. "Rear guard," Tim said. The point man led them along the trail. They came around a turn; the point man had halted them, then gestured them forward.

"Look at that!" Tim said. "I think that's the Kraut you shot."

David and Tim stopped. A dead man lay beside the trail, silver braid on his grey uniform. His tunic was pulled open and the man's white shirt – a buttoned dress shirt, to David's surprise – was bloody. There was a bandage tied around his chest.

David examined the dead German. The braid on the grey uniform looked familiar. "I guess all their officers look kind of alike," he thought. "But this." There was a piece of a black cross made of heavy metal, clipped to the man's left breast pocket. Three arms of a Maltese cross and a fragment of the junction. The black arms of the cross were edged with silver and there was a design in the shattered junction. There was a bullet hole about where the cross would have hung. "My shot? Yes, my shot. God, I pray you have his soul with you now. I had to do it. He was going to kill my buddies."

"Hey, that's a cool souvenir," Tim said.

"Souvenir. To remember," David answered. To himself he said, "Why do I want this? To show I triumphed? To show I can kill? No. God, I'm sorry I killed him. I'm sorry I had to do it. Let me think of that every time I look at this. This wasn't a sin but it was still terrible.

"For Your sake I became a coastie instead of a soldier. And here I am and here he is. What did that damned Hitler cost him?" David took the cross off of the dead man's pocket and put it with the two dog tags he had. "My pocket has become the picture of irony," he thought.

Tim was kneeling beside the dead officer. "Looks like his Luger is already gone. Maybe one of his own men took it." Tim did get the Luger's holster off the dead man's belt and pushed it into his own belt. "I hope I can hang onto it," he said.

"Get your asses moving up here," the sergeant shouted back at them. They resumed their way up the trail. They were at a concrete gun emplacement. The gun was torn apart and one dead man lay in the pit. "Looks like the Navy got this one, anyway," the captain said.

"We're behind the German line, it looks like. Look at all these trenches. Now watch out. We've got no good idea where these go and who may still be in them." There was machine-gun fire coming from a point a hundred yards or so along the trench lines and the patrol began to move toward it.

A shell whistled overhead and exploded somewhere past the apparent location of the nest. "Well, damn it. If the Navy keeps trying to get that one, they'll get us instead," the captain said.

Shells continued to whistle overhead and struck further west, closer to where most of the German firing seemed to be. "A lot less noise here. I can almost hear myself think."

The captain said, "Let's get going." David fell back to the rear with Tim as they moved through the trench. The point man had his rifle at his shoulder and the captain was behind him and to his right; the captain had his .45 in his right hand and forward also. As they approached the Widerstand, they heard voices ahead – voices raised in anger and maybe in fear. There was a scuffling sound, a shot, and then more talking. "I know French and a little German. That's some other language. Could these be Russians?" As they moved toward the pillbox, the point man raised his rifle's muzzle. Four men came out of the pillbox, hands raised. "Kamerad, kamerad," one of them said.

"What is this all about?" the point man asked the captain.

"That's a good question," David thought. One of the soldiers motioned the four men away from the pillbox's entrance. A dead German lay on the floor. David was astonished at the appearance of the four men – dark skin, slanted eyes, German uniforms.

"Kamerad! Amerikanish? Amerikanish?" said one of the four men.

"We're Americans," the captain said. "Do any of you speak English?"

"Kein Anglische," said one of the men. "Bissen Deutsche." The captain nodded. One of the men who'd come with him said, "I speak bissen Deutsche, cap'n. Shall I try?"

"Go ahead," the captain said. "I think I know what the story is."

There was a slow, awkward exchange of German. The phrase "nicht soldaten" came up repeatedly and the obvious "nicht Deutsche." The word "hanguk" came up a few times also. The translator reported, "My German is thin and theirs is worse, but they're from some place way east, past Russia or maybe Siberia. Some place called Hanguk and these men are Hans but I've never heard of it."

"We can send these guys down to the beach. They're Osties – men from the East. They got captured in other areas and drafted into the German army."

David understood now. "These poor guys got dragged in worse than I did. Long way from home and I bet the German sergeants are a lot harder than CPOs. These men figured out we were coming and they managed to jump the German who was keeping them here."

"Cap'n, do you want me to send an escort?"

"No, sergeant. These men just want out. That beach is still really bad. They can take their chances heading down. I need all of our rifles here. Corporal, does your bissen Deutche extend to asking about a white flag?"

"Sure, cap'n." There was another difficult exchange and one of the Asian soldiers produced a white cloth. They fastened it to a rod. "Tell them to keep waving this as they go down," the captain said. "That may keep our boys from shooting them. If they meet a German patrol, they're going to be in a bad fix but this is all we can do for them."

The sergeant was examining the machine-gun. "We gotta put this out of action like the last one, cap'n," he said. "Strip it," he said to the soldier who had disabled the previous gun.

"Right, sarge," he said. A few moments later he was passing out the parts for souvenirs. "Hey, private, I missed your name before."

The man who had bent the barrel on the other machine gun answered, "Belden, Michael M."

"Do your strongman act again, would ya?" The private proceeded to smash the barrel of the machine gun against the floor until is was bent and useless.

They went to examine the pillbox. David put part of the bolt into his pocket with the dog tags. "Three dead men and a dead machine gun," he said to himself. "And I still need to take a leak."

The whole patrol seemed to have reached that conclusion; men were relieving themselves against the concrete walls. Afterward, they drank from canteens.

"Hell of a morning," the captain said. "We can hope the day gets better but I'm betting it won't, boys. Time to move out."

David stood up with the patrol. He was surprised to find his legs aching. "We've been working harder than I thought." All of the men seemed stiff for a few moments. They continued down the trenches. Perhaps the captain had some idea of where they were headed; all David could tell was that they were moving back toward the west, toward the more intense fighting. "We've had the best of it so far," David realized. "Everywhere is bad, but things get tougher as we move west."

David watched the beach for a few minutes as they moved along. More landing craft had brought more men. There was more wreckage on the beach and in the water. Landing craft were circling at some distance. "They're loaded but the beach is too much of a mess to land. Everyone is bogged down. Good God, be with them all. There's a lot of bodies out there. Bring the wounded in safely, please, God. Bring the dead to you. German or American or…Osties, did the captain say?" He was shocked to realize that he'd forgotten his own crew. "God, please bring the guys home. And the wounded man who was in the well. Home on earth, home with You. Please be with them."

The patrol continued along the trench. They found another pillbox; one of the destroyers had found it first. The bunker contained an appalling stew. "Direct hit, I guess," David said.

"These pillboxes are smaller and thinner than the big gun emplacements," the captain said. "The shell managed to blow this one apart."

Tim muttered a few harsh words. "This is like the back room at the butcher shop," he said. "But the steers didn't wear boots."

"Or helmets," said David. He knelt beside some of the wreckage, mechanical and human. "God, them too," he said. "How many do you think there were?"

"The parts are awfully messed up. The other nest had four men – the Kraut doesn't count. So probably four men here too. Well, we can move out. No idea if they were really Germans or some poor dragooned guys."

"Dragooned guys. Osties. Men from way East of here. They disappeared and their families don't know anything about what happened to them. God, be with their families and mine. All of our families."

They continued through the trenches. "Hey, Tim, we're on top of the bluff," David said.

"You missed that, huh? Yeah, we've been on top for a while now."

"God, thank You for safety this far," David said to himself. They heard firing ahead, clearly another automatic weapon that was still out of sight. The captain was speaking.

"Almost have to be Krauts. Most of our guys with heavy stuff are still trying to get off the beach, it looks like. But we need to be sure before we engage. It's too damned easy to shoot our buddies or them to shoot us."

David marched with the patrol. They saw another pillbox firing. The captain motioned them all down. He and sergeant conferred; the machine gun crew in the pillbox apparently hadn't seen them. The sergeant came over in a belly crawl and explained the plan.

"We're going to try the same thing. We should be able to put some shots through the embrasure there. Then I'm going to get a grenade in there and we'll see what that does."

"Everyone looks kind of doubtful," David thought to himself.

"We haven't been spotted yet but it'll happen pretty soon. Form a line and everyone fires when I do."

"Those guys are so focused on the beach, they've missed us coming right on top of them," David thought. He sighted carefully on the embrasure opening. It was about twenty yards away. "Pretty easy shot with an M-1," he thought. "Watch your own shots."

The sergeant fired and the patrol began firing. David fired. "That one's high. Shift. Take a moment." He fired again. "No dust from the concrete, no dirt, probably about right." He continued to fire and suddenly the empty clip was flying. "Action's open. Safety. New clip down the top. Let the action go. Keep your thumb out of the way."

The squad had quit firing; so had the machine gun crew. The sergeant crawled forward with startling speed. His first grenade missed the embrasure and blasted, apparently harmlessly, on the ground in front of the pillbox. "That could get one of us killed," David thought. The next grenade went right into the embrasure and went off a few seconds later.

The men rushed the pillbox but there was still no firing. They found the entrance. The captain went in with his .45 forward and the point man followed him. They motioned the others to come in a moment later.

A German soldier slumped against the back wall. His pistol was on the floor beside him but he was making no effort to pick it up or use it. His tunic was bloody and torn up; he gasped a few times and then was silent. Three other Germans were dead on the floor. "At least I assume they're Germans – they were fighting hard," David thought. The pillbox stank of gunpowder fumes, hot metal, the explosive from the grenade and the blood of their enemies that spattered every surface of the pillbox.

David was appalled all over again. "Oh, God, what have I done? What have we all done? Our duty, sure, but what wretched duty. Please gather their souls, God. Please let this be our last sip from this cup. But there will be more, I'm sure."

"The gun's ruined," the captain said. "Let's move out."

As they moved closer, the captain suddenly halted them and motioned them down. "Those gunners saw us. They're watching this direction. We'll have to take them somehow. They're in a foxhole nest instead of a pillbox so it ought to be easier."

The sergeant and the captain gave their orders. "We'll toss a couple of grenades and then rush after they go off. Sometimes the grenades do the whole job and they'll rattle the Germans at least."

"The Germans are tracking us," Tim said. Every few seconds a burst would go overhead. "They're aiming, not just tossing random bursts." David realized that the gun crew meant to drive them off or kill them. Their patrol had to act, though. Men on the beach were being killed.

David would have gotten in another prayer but he heard the pins and spoons. He saw the men tossing the grenades. There was a ragged series of blasts. "Go, go, go," the sergeant yelled. "Get moving!"

The men ran through the smoke and dust. Dropping into the foxhole, David found himself in a melee but it was brief. The Germans were dead, at least one from a knife slice to his throat. A GI was down too – one of the men whom David didn't know, who had come with the captain. David knelt beside him. "The soldiers know the shooting business and I know this job," he said, wondering if the man could even hear him. Blood on his jacket and a separate area on his right thigh, high up. "I miss Dad's knife. This belt I picked up has a bayonet. Cut his clothes and let's see what we've got." David ripped the wounded man's jacket open first, praying beyond words for God to coach him. "Okay, it's rough. He's got a slash across his stomach but everything's still inside. Where's his field dressing?" Hands held out the packages. David started with the sulfa, the powder that could help save the young man's life by protecting him from infection. Then he pressed the large dressing against the gash and, with the help of men to roll the wounded man, tied it as tightly as he could. "I hope everything missed his spinal cord or he may never walk again," David said.

"Let's see your leg," he said, still thinking the man was too weak to hear him. "Doc?" the man whispered.

"Yeah, buddy?" he asked. No point in explanations.

"How bad is my leg?"

David ripped the bloody pants open. "It's another bad gash."

"Are my balls there?" David almost laughed.

"Yes, the cut is a couple of inches below." "This is a really scary wound. Way up high, bleeding like a stuck pig." "Gotta tie this down," he said out loud. More sulfa, then the bandage in the kit. David was still scared. "Is there a sling bandage in there?" he asked. Tim handed it to him. "Okay, buddy, hold on." David leaned his full weight on the gash and the wounded man writhed. "I know, it hurts like crazy, but I've got to do it." Holding on as hard as he could, he worked with the others to tie the sling bandage, folded into a strip, around the man's leg. "Tourniquet? No, too high. Will he keep this leg? God, be with him."

"Oh, God, it hurts."

"We can do something about that," David said. He found the man's morphine syrettes and injected one into his left arm. Then he hooked the needle of the syrette through the flap on the man's shirt pocket.

"Captain, this man has to get back to the beach."

"Damnation. If we try to take him down, we'll lose at least two men with him and we might kill him when we tried to get him down that bluff. There will be casualty aid stations up here pretty soon. I hope there will be, anyway. We're going to have to bring him with us the best way we can. Sailor, we'll make that your job – yours and Moore's."

Two of the men had found ponchos in the machine-gun nest. "Here's some kind of netting as well. The net will provide handles for us to carry the wounded man. Let's lay out the ponchos so it's a little more comfortable." The men used bayonets to cut out a rough stretcher.

The sergeant was arranging the patrol. "Mallory's kinda small," he said. "The trenches are too narrow to make a four-man carry team so it's going to have to be you and sailor, Moore."

"This'd be easier if we had poles," David said.

"This will work. The net is all we have so we'll do our best with what we've got."

The sergeant looked at David a moment. "Sailor, I think I understand you some. I can see you trying to carry Mallory too long. Listen, this is an order. If you get tired, you say so and I'll put another man on. That's for Mallory's sake and everyone's. If you fall out while you're carrying him, it'll be a mess. If you have to slow down, we'll all be slowed down. So listen up and tell me when you need a change. You, too, Moore, but I know you'll gripe when you get tired."

The patrol took up positions. David and Tim, carrying Mallory on the improvised litter, were in the middle. A corporal was on point and a private had rear guard. They continued working to the west.

Several men in German uniforms approached, waving a white flag. "Speak English?" the captain asked.

"Yes, English. Vee are Russians," said one of the men. "Kamerad."

"If you're Russians, you're probably happy to sell out the Germans. What can you tell me about what's up ahead?" the captain asked.

"We saw American patrol that way," the Russian said, pointing vaguely west. "Next two guns, all Germans. Good hunting." The captain nodded and waved the group of men toward the beach. "They're in a bad fix whatever happens," he said. "If they get back to Russia, they may get shot as traitors."

As the patrol moved east, they heard exchanges of gunfire. "I'm catching on," David said. "The machine guns sound different from our Tommy guns."

"Damn few Tommies up here anyway," Tim said. "Some of the squads have BARs. They'll fire in very short bursts because the gunners have to reload pretty fast. The BARs sound different from the German guns too."

A whistle put all of the men on the ground. "Incoming!" someone yelled. An explosion tore up the ground about ten yards away; shrapnel sang around them.

David lifted his head slightly. The captain was talking with the sergeant. The sergeant snaked over to them. "There's a mortar position to our left and we've got to take it out." Another whistle, another explosion. "That seemed closer," David said to Tim.

"They're trying to walk the rounds in on us. The Krauts must have a lot of mortar shells, using 'em to try to take out a squad like us."

The patrol was crawling on their bellies toward the mortar pit. "They can arc pretty good but I think we're inside their arc now," Tim said. Helmeted heads would pop up and fire a few rounds from rifles; soldiers fired back. A tube-shaped grenade came flying and David tried to push himself right through the ground, but the weapon failed. They waited a minute to be sure it was a dud and then Tim tossed it into some bushes.

"That happens a lot," Tim said. "Intel thinks maybe the slave workers in the ammo plants are sabotaging the grenades. Something sure is making a lot of them duds. But you have to treat them as live until you're sure."

The men closest to the mortar pit were tossing grenades. Again a flurry of explosions; this time there were screams and grunts after the grenades went off.

There was no shooting from the pit. "Come on," the captain said and rose. They ran to the pit, crouched. "This again," David thought as he looked at the wreckage. "And this." He knelt by a German whose front was torn apart and bloody. The man vomited on him just as David was trying to see if he could help him. Then he slumped back, eyes open and glazed. "He just died," David realized. "I've seen that before. God, take his soul, please. Bring him to You."

"This whole crew is dead," the sergeant said. "What about the mortar?"

"Pack it with dirt. I doubt the Germans will be back here at all; I haven't seen any sign of them really counter-attacking, just holding on where they are. If we fill the mortar with dirt, it'll take a crew a long time to put it back in action if they do come along." A couple of the men used their trenching tools to pack the mortar and they moved off.

"Someone ahead of us, cap'n," said the point man. "I think they're speaking English."

"Everyone freeze," the captain said. "Be ready but be slow to shoot. We could be in a firefight with our own guys unless we're careful."

"I can hear the boots now," David said to himself. The point man was calling out, "Americans here! Who's that?"

A few moments later they had linked up with an American patrol. There were a couple of tense moments as they made sure of who was whom. A sergeant from the 29th was leading the patrol they met. "How did you get here?" the captain asked. "This is Big Red One territory."

"Fortunes of war, cap'n," the sergeant answered. "I picked up a few men and we kept trying to find our way up. And here we are."

"I'm going to take command, then. Your team will be second squad."

"Yes, sir."

An enormous cloud of dust and debris erupted well to the west. Seconds later a roaring sound pushed them all to the bottom of the trench. "What the hell was that?" the new sergeant asked.

They all popped their heads up for a look. Grazing fire pushed them right back down. The captain braved the grazing fire and got a look through his binoculars. He put the binoculars back inside his jacket.

"There was a big wall at the west end of the landing area," he said. "'Was' being the operative word. I think it was holding up the men on the beach, getting them killed. Anyway, instead of a wall, now there's a lot of concrete blocks and ways through them. The Navy may have blown it or maybe the engineers did. That's going to be a big deal. There are a lot of those barriers. Blowing them is going to be crucial.

"We need to keep working our way west. That gun that was trying to scalp me has to be silenced." David knew that meant the crew had to be killed unless they surrendered. So far, only Osties had surrendered.

The patrol moved along the trench. Everyone was crouched. The captain was talking with the private on point. "Son, I'm going to take point for a while. The Germans may be probing this trench and we'll meet suddenly if they are. I think my .45 is a better weapon for the job right now. You stay close up behind me. Corporal, you and the sailor keep the wounded man toward the rear but be ready to put him down and shoot. Rear guard!"

"Yeah, cap'n?"

"Same thing. If we get in trouble from your direction, yell 'scatter' if you're scared." The captain paused. "Well, hell, we're all scared. More scared, son, know what I mean?"

The private at the rear grinned a moment. "Yes, sir, I think I do," he answered.

"Sarge, how are we fixed for grenades?"

The sergeants went along the patrol. "We've got six left."

"That's pretty thin. We'll try to save them for bigger problems if we can."

"That's a pretty dubious look," David thought as he saw the sergeant grimace. "Sarge thinks it's going to be tough to take the next nest with just rifles."

They approached the next machine-gun nest. "I thought the Germans fought their machine guns in pillboxes," David said to Tim.

"Oh, sure, mostly they do. But ya gotta have mobility and be flexible, even if you're a damn Kraut from a dictatorship. So some of the guns are in more open places, like that mortar we cleared out."

As they moved forward, the captain stayed ahead with his sidearm ready. Suddenly he pointed it and fired twice. The squad moved up behind him; a German lay dead in front of him. "Straggler of some kind," the captain said. They moved past him and found themselves by the machine-gun nest. The captain said "Halt" and David and Tom set their improvised litter down.

David popped his head up for a moment. "The Germans must have missed that we were coming up," he thought. "They're all looking toward the beach." That meant they were aiming at the soldiers down there or perhaps some working their way up the bluffs. The gun had to be silenced, just like the last one.

"We're going to try to surprise them and shoot them instead of using the grenades." The captain saw the look on the sergeant's face. "Yes, it's risky. I'd rather call in a shell or use the grenades but we're going to need them."

"Captain, maybe I can do something," David said. "Do you think I can stand up for about thirty seconds?"

"Dicey, son. You can hear all the shooting and if those Germans figure out we're here, they'll mow you like grass on Saturday morning."

"I can try to wig-wag a destroyer and see about calling in a barrage."

The captain gave that some thought. "No, sailor, I like your thinking but we'll have to solve our own problem. You're liable to be killed before you get the message clear and we're too close anyway. Even a direct hit might get us too and a miss probably would get us. War is like that."

David nodded. Even with precise coordinates, and he could not provide those, a shell might hit near but not on the nest. "And 'near' could only too easily be right in our laps."

"We're going to try a stealthy approach," the captain said. "They all look kind of glum at that idea," David noticed. "Sailor, you're going to stay here with Mallory. Try to watch what we're doing in case you have to try this next time yourself. But your main job is rear guard." The captain picked four men. "Belly crawl right to the edge and give them hell," he said. "The rest of us will come through the trench and burst in as you get the party going. Everybody make sure who you're shooting, now."

"Well, I guess that's a plan," Tim muttered. He moved forward to join the rest of the patrol and the rear guard moved up. "You got the rear now," the private said. David nodded and knelt, braced and facing the trench where they had come from.

Noise. Gunshots, cries that David couldn't understand. Sudden shouting from the direction he was facing and two men in German uniforms were rushing toward him. He fired rapidly; there were four rounds in the clip and it made a metallic sproing sound as it flew out. The Garand was empty. He put it down and went over.

David looked at the two men down in front of him. "I never even sighted," he said to himself. But they were down, all right. One was trying to reach for his rifle. David jumped forward and stomped on the German's hand. He bent and snatched the rifle away, then threw it as far as he could. "Stay put," he said, doubting the German understood. He knelt on top of the injured man and took the rifle from the other man's hand. There was no response or resistance. "Well, that one's dead too," David said to himself. "I should feel bad but I'm just relieved."

Tim and the rear guard had just returned. "Krauts in the nest are kaput," Tim said. "What happened here?"

"The very thing you thought could happen," David said. "A couple of Germans came up behind and I stopped them." The words "shot" and "killed" somehow stuck in his throat.

"Your bolt's open," Tim said. David nodded and pulled a clip from his ammo pouch. Tim put on the safety, pushed the clip down and released the bolt. "Okay, you got one in the chamber now," Tim said.

The German at his feet moaned. David and Tim turned him over. "Right above the heart, I think," David thought. "He might get over this."

The captain had come back. "What do we do with him?" David asked, pointing to the wounded German.

"We can patch him and then we'll have to abandon him. I know it's cruel, but we have to abandon him or kill him outright and I won't do that." the captain said, responding to David's look. "We have too few men to carry him to safety or guard him. Get a bandage on him and we'll hope his people find him. Another American patrol may find him and bring him in. He might live through this."

David and Tim quickly put the German's own bandage over his wound. The man watched them with angry and distrustful eyes. "Well, I'd be like that," said David to himself. The German was also muttering; their makeshift translator chuckled.

"I'll give you the details later if you want them," he said. "They are just as complimentary as you think they are."

David finished tying the bandage with a rueful smile. "I'd have left you in peace gladly," he said to the German, knowing the wounded man wouldn't get the words. He touched the translator. "How would I say, 'God be with you'?"

"'Gott mitt zee' is as close as I can get," the translator said. "Why?"

David had bent low over the wounded German. "Gott mitt zee," he said. The German glared. Two of the men frisked the German to be sure he had no weapons left and the patrol formed up.

One of the soldiers took the bolt out of one of the German rifles. He drove the bayonet into the ground and draped the dead German's coat over it. "Marker for someone to find these guys," he said as David watched him curiously. Another soldier had collected the working rifle.

David took up the foot of the improvised litter again. The translator had taken Tim's place at the head; that meant David was in front because they were carrying Mallory feet-first. Blood had seeped through the bandage on Mallory's thigh and on his belly as well. "God be with you also, friend," David whispered.

The patrol moved along the trench. They continued in silence for what seemed a long time. David's watch was stopped and his sense of time was shot. "That's hard to explain," David said to himself. "I'm scared and bored at the same time. How does that work?"

The captain's watch was working, apparently. "It's just about noon," he said. "This is as quiet as things are likely to get, so we're going to take twenty minutes to rest and eat. Sailor, check the pouches on your belt. There may be some food in there. Slim chance, most of us carry rations in our pockets."

David checked the pouches. "No, sir, nothing."

"All right, let's see who has what. Who's got a little to share?"

Tim handed over a "B" pack. "Crackers and candy, better than nothin'." Another soldier gave him an "M" unit. "I've given my hounds better dog food than this, but it'll keep you going." He had opened the can with his small can opener. David dug in with his fingers to get the beef hash. "I need to be careful or I'll slice my fingers on that edge," he thought. "That'd be a stupid thing to do today."

David noticed that every other man had begun to eat before the captain opened his own rations. "Make sure you drink," the captain said. "No smoking yet. The scent of tobacco could draw trouble."

The sergeant spoke quietly with the captain. "Sarge has sold me. One cigarette if you want."

David and the others ate quickly. Tim extended a cigarette toward David. "That's quite an offer, Tim. I know how hard they are to get. Thanks so much, but I don't smoke."

Tim nodded. "Guys who talk as soft as you rarely do."

The patrol completed their break in what passed for quiet. David wetted Mallory's lips from a canteen. "If we try to help him drink, he'll choke," he said to Tim. "And if his gut is torn up, water could leak into his belly."

Tim nodded. "This is all we can do until we get him to an aid station." They exchanged looks; they both realized that Mallory's chance of living that long was thin.

"One more thing," David said. He put his hand lightly on Mallory's forehead – it was cool and damp, the man was in shock. "The Lord is my shepherd," David began, and quickly recited the full psalm.

"Prayer gonna help him?" Tim asked. "Lot of unanswered prayers around us, David."

"Maybe the prayer is to help us help him," David said. "Maybe God will put His hand here."

"Listen up, everyone. Make sure your hands are as clean as you can get them. Grease from the food will make your hands slippery. Use your pants or your sleeves, but clean your hands off," the sergeant ordered. They lifted their net and their burden gently and moved off.

Half an hour passed. David remembered his orders as his shoulders ached. "Sergeant," he called. "You said I should ask for relief. I think I need it."

"Sure. Keep moving, though. Who's right in front of sailor? Take his place."

The soldier got a grip on the netting as they marched. David let go. "Thanks, shipmate," he said.

"Shipmate?" the soldier asked.

"Hey, if I'm going to be 'sailor', you can all be 'shipmate'," David answered. "Tim's name is the only one I've caught."

"I could use a relief too," Tim was saying. The soldier behind him took up the load without an order and Tim moved back into his place. All this time they had been moving through the German-dug trenches slowly. Every turn was a danger, every intersection, but the march was going quietly. "First time I remember being this bored and this scared at the same time," David said to the soldier at Mallory's feet.

"My first day in combat too," the soldier answered. "Tim and sarge and the captain, I think they're the only ones who have been in combat."

"I've been in landings – Sicily and Salerno. I've been shot at before. This is the first time I've been in a fix like this, though. Since the only thing that'll break up the boredom is more fighting, I'll be glad to be bored," David said. The soldier nodded and they plodded on.

The captain raised his hand in a halt gesture but didn't say the command. The patrol shuffled to a stop. The captain gestured and they all crouched. He continued using hand signals instead of spoken orders. David looked at the soldier in front of him, a man with corporal's stripes. As David opened his mouth, the soldier put his hand to his lips and David nodded. "Silence, worth four dollars a minute," he thought to himself, remembering a Twain story. The point man had moved ahead in the trench and was out of sight.

There were clicks around David as soldiers took off their safeties. The point man returned and whispered urgently to the captain. There was a game of telephone down the patrol and David got his orders. "Sailor, you stay here with Mallory. We've got problems up ahead." The patrol members behind David moved around him and the wounded man, as quietly as they could, and a minute later David was alone with Mallory. The wounded man was breathing roughly but quietly enough. "What am I going to do if he starts to moan or talk?" David asked himself.

"They've been gone a long time," David thought, though a working watch would have shown him it was only about two minutes. The wait ended with bursts of gunfire. The sounds were wildly confused; David thought he heard an automatic weapon chattering as well as rapid fire from the Garands. Shouting, rough language in English, German phrases. Silence again.

David could hear the sound of boots approaching – "Whose boots?" he asked himself. He eased the safety off of his rifle but kept the muzzle pointed into the ground of the trench. When the boots seemed close he whispered, "Who goes there? I'm ready to shoot."

"Friend, sailor."

"Anyone could say friend, but only someone from our patrol would know I was 'sailor.'" David eased the safety back on and a corporal came around the bend in the trench.

"We had a dustup. Four Krauts dead and another of our guys is shot up. Let's go." David took the head end of their improvised litter and the corporal took the foot. Standing, they moved quickly to the point where the patrol was crouched again.

"Sailor, how are you doing as doc?" the sergeant asked.

"I'm a better corpsman than I am a rifleman," he said.

"You and Moore see what you can do for the private here."

The man was seated on the floor of the trench and propped against the wall. He had a patch of blood on the front of his shirt just below his right collar bone. David helped him open his shirt; the entrance wound was a furrow rather than a circle. David leaned him forward; there was an exit wound, rather larger than the entrance. There was an ugly sound of air coming from each of the wounds.

"Sucking chest wound," David said.

"Yeah, figured that out," the wounded man said. "I can feel my chest squeezing. I can move my arms so I think my spine is okay." The only injury that frightened men more than being paralyzed was being castrated.

David shook half of the man's sulfa into the front wound and the rest into the back. Instead of using the gauze from the bandages, he used their plastic wrappers against the wounds and then the gauze over the plastic. "That should help with the air coming in," he told the wounded man.

"A little, I guess," the man said. He was taking short, gasping breaths. "This'll sound like something from a movie, but don't try to talk," David said. "You're going to need all your breath."

David spoke to the sergeant. "I'm not a corpsman but I know this man's in a bad way. I'm trying to figure out the best way to carry him."

"What's the problem?"

"If we carry him flat, like we're doing for Mallory, he'll likely drown in his own blood. If he tries to walk, he'll breathe harder and there's bound to be a hole in his lung besides the two outside on his chest. We should try to carry him propped up and I'm not sure how to do it."

The sergeant looked doubtful. "Which'd be easier for him? To be carried flat or to try to walk?"

David shook his head. "I don't know. Both of these men need to get to an aid station."

"Well, no crap, sailor. I have no idea where an aid station is yet." The sergeant spoke with the captain, so low that David missed the conversation. Then he came back and spoke to the man with the chest wounds.

"Son, you're going to have to walk, it looks like. We'll stop when you need to. And you tell me when you need to; if you wear yourself out, you'll make us a lot slower than if we stop every ten minutes or so." The soldier nodded and the sergeant helped him stand. "Can't shoot like this," he gasped. David suddenly found himself with a second rifle on his left shoulder. They moved out again. The patrol was moving about as fast as it had been because they'd had to move slowly with Mallory on his stretcher; the second wounded man was able to keep pace.

But every few minutes the man with the chest wound would have to tap the captain on his shoulder and the squad would halt for a minute while he got his breath again. The intervals grew shorter as they moved west toward the main body of the invasion force.

From time to time the captain would scan the beach and the bluff with his binoculars. "Blowing that wall made a lot of difference and the first guys are just now getting on top of the bluff," he said. "I think they've blown some more of the obstacles. It's good new; we're probably half a mile from linking up with them."

"Does it look like they've started to set up aid stations?" David asked.

"No way to know, sailor. I don't see any Red Cross flags yet. Thing is, we may spot a Red Cross and find out it's Kraut."

"It might be worth it, getting these guys some help even if they become prisoners."

"It won't just be them, though. The whole patrol would be captured or we'd have to surrender. We've got to get through to our own lines and our own people."

David shook his head. "That calculus seems wrong," he thought, "but the captain is in command. Mine to obey, not question."

The patrol trudged on through the trenches. "Here it is again," David thought. "Bored and terrified at the same time."

Mallory on his stretcher was breathing in very shallow breaths. "You look like Hell," David said to himself. The man with the chest wounds was clearly using the last of his own resources to try to keep up. David moved up to speak to the sergeant.

"Our walking wounded is only going to hold out a few more minutes," David said.

"Yeah, I can see that."

"I'll carry him a while. Everyone else has gear on his back, so I'm the best guy to do it. He's kind of small. If I hand these rifles off, I think I can back-pack him for a while. That's the only way to carry him; if we try a shoulder carry, we'll stop him breathing at all."

The sergeant looked dubious but he nodded. "We're getting to desperate times and desperate measures," he said to David "Halt!" he called to the patrol. "Ten minutes unless the Krauts do something."

All of the men sagged down. They drank some water and collected themselves. At the end of the break, the sergeant said to the man with the chest wounds, "The sailor is going to carry you a while."

"What do you mean?" the man protested. His gasping speech and a spit of blood belied his protest.

"We'll go faster that way and the sailor's no dogface to start with. So he's the cheapest rifle to lose." When the wounded man opened his mouth, the sergeant raised his hand to stop him. "I'm telling you, soldier. We're bringing you with us and this is the best way to do it."

As they organized to march again, David got a length of some kind of webbed strap from one of the soldiers – he had no idea where it had come from. Among them, they got the wounded man onto David's back and used the webbing to tie his legs in front. "Can you drop that strap quick if you need to?" the sergeant asked.

"Yes," David said after testing the knot.

"You gonna be okay, soldier? You, sailor?" Both men nodded. "Move out," the sergeant said.

Behind David and his passenger were the two men carrying Mallory. All the men were silent – fatigue, tension, and combat doctrine combined to hush them.

Rather suddenly the trench sloped up and they found themselves on the bluff again. A few hundred yards ahead was a group of men. "Going by their helmets and uniforms, they should be Americans," David thought. The captain hailed them.

"Prove you're Americans," the man in front of the new group said.

"What kind of Germans have a Coast Guard guy with them?" the captain asked and pointed at David.

"You'll do. What kind of proof do you want?"

"How many times has Franklin Roosevelt been elected president?"

"Three."

"That'll do, too."

The two groups came together. One of the men in the new group was a medic, armband and all. "Looks like my turn," he said.

The medic took a quick look at the man that David was carrying, then knelt where the litter-bearers had set Mallory on the ground. He took quick looks at each of the wounded men. "They're both in bad ways," he said. "You've done as much for these men as I could've done and undoing their bandages would make things worse."

"Any aid stations yet?"

"Yes, sir, about four hundred yards that direction," the medic said and pointed further west, "There's a Red Cross tarp on a barn. You'll see it around that turn."

The captain was speaking with the lieutenant in command of the unit they had linked up with. "Here's the plan, men. Moore, you and the sailor are going to go to the aid station with the wounded men. You both need a look yourselves. The rest of us will proceed inland and east again, back where we came from but moving in. Moore, you stay at the aid station and we'll get word to you where to rejoin us. We should put one more man on the litter with Mallory, though."

The soldier with the chest wound gasped. "I'm bad off but I can walk that far, cap'n. I'm rested some."

"All right. You four are the only injured men we have and I want to keep everyone else. Moore, you take the litter with sailor. Stay at the aid station until we send word or you hear about where units are regrouping. Sailor, the people at the aid station will find a way to get you back to your ship." The captain paused a moment longer. "But do this for me, sailor. Write me out your name and your unit." The captain produced a notebook and a pencil and David wrote out his information. "I may have a chance to notify your unit where you are before you do."

The sergeant shook David's hand. "You been a good soldier, for a sailor," he said. "Your road goes back to your ship now; our way home goes through Berlin."

"God be with you," David said, holding the sergeant's hand in both of his. "God be with you."

"Et cum spiritu tuo."

David smiled. "I know you have a long way to go. So that makes you a roaming Catholic." The sergeant smiled and nodded.

The Aid Station

The patrol moved out along the bluff. David and Tim carried Mallory on the litter. The soldier with the chest wound leaned on Tim some. "Hurts like hell but I can keep going," he said. "I have to now."

Ten trudging minutes brought them to the barn with its tarp. "Now that's a sight I wanted to see," David said as they approached. A soldier stopped them. "Make me believe you're Americans," he said.

"I've got two wounded men and we all have GI dog tags on," David answered. They all produced their dog tags and the guard waved them into the barn. The light was dim but there were many flashlights and a couple of lanterns in use. There was human wreckage all around; some voices groaned and some spoke. There was cursing everywhere, some spitting sounds and what sounded like vomiting in some places. Pleas for mothers, for women who might be wives or girlfriends, murmurs of prayer.

A medic and a doctor met them. "Let's get you onto a stretcher," the medic said to the man with the chest wound.

"He's sucking air through his chest," David said.

The medic led him to a litter that had some boxes at the head. The boxes were draped with blankets for padding. The blankets were bright quilts, though. "Yeah, some of the French mothers have brought us blankets and things," the medic said. "This will prop him up." The medic helped the man sit on the litter and David brought his legs up. Another medic was cutting the injured man's shirt away. He swabbed the man's elbow with an alcohol wipe; David could smell the fumes. The injured man swore for a moment as the medic jabbed a large needle into his elbow and started plasma running to his vein. "Help me a minute," the medic said and they taped the man's arm to a small board to keep it straight.

David got the soldier's boots off. The wounded man gasped, "Thanks, sailor."

The doctor was listening to the man's chest. The bloody shirt and undershirt had been cut away and lay on the floor. "That was good work," the doctor said, looking at the gauze and plastic. He was swabbing the man's upper chest with antiseptic as David turned away to see what had happened to Mallory.

Another doctor was kneeling on the dirt floor and listening to Mallory's chest with a stethoscope. David felt a cold knot in his chest. "Yes, just what we feared," he said as the doctor shook his head. He pointed to another area of the barn. Tim and David used the makeshift litter to carry Mallory over.

"Of course; this is the morgue," David realized. The bodies were laid on the floor; each body lay on a blanket that would be used later to move the dead man. The blankets were folded over the dead men. "Stretchers are at a premium," David realized. "They'll be reserved for moving and holding the living."

"Let's set Mallory down," David said. "We can leave him on this; it will do to move him. Let's cover him, though." David knelt beside the dead man. He took Mallory's hand and recited. "Our Father, Who art in Heaven, hallowed be Thy Name. Thy Kingdom come, Thy will be done, on Earth as it is in Heaven. Give us this day our daily bread and forgive us our trespasses as we forgive those who trespass against us. Lead us not into temptation, but deliver us from evil. For Thine is the Kingdom and the power and the glory forever. Please give our brother Mallory grace and hold him in Your eternal embrace. Amen." They draped Mallory's corpse.

"How did a Navy chaplain get here?" a soldier asked.

"David's from the Coast Guard. And he's not a chaplain, he's just a boat driver," Tim said.

"That's right," David said softly, distractedly. "Anyone can pray. All of us had better pray."

David and several others went outside. There was some bustle around a table and it had the look of administrative work. "Paper pushers," Tim said as they headed in that direction.

"Somebody has to keep track of what's going on," David said. They went to the table. One of the soldiers with a clipboard approached. "Soldiers, I need your names and tell me what we need to do for you."

"Moore, Timothy, corporal. Got a graze on my shoulder."

"Ryerson, David, bosun's mate third class, from the Chase. I've gotten separated from my ship and I've got a cut on my scalp."

"Separated? You sure are. We'll try to get word to your ship. Let's get your wound seen to first. See the group under the trees there? Minor injuries. You okay otherwise, I guess?"

"Yes, but I've got something else." David fished in his pocket and brought out the two dog tags. "These are tags of men I know are dead."

The man with the clipboard took the two tags. "I'll get these to Graves Registration," he said. "Do you know where the bodies are?"

"Not really. One was underwater as I came in. I'm betting he's lost at sea. The other was on the beach."

"You did right to get the tags like you did. You're probably right about the man who was underwater being lost and the man on the beach may be lost too. You go over and get your wounds checked."

"There were three other men on my boat. And a wounded soldier. I guess there's no way to check on their situation, is there?"

The soldier with the clipboard gave a bitter guffaw. "You're right about that. Twenty thousand men came ashore this morning and more are coming now. Hardly anybody knows where he is himself, let alone anyone else. We're getting word to some central points but there's nothing coming back."

The aid station was in an area that passed for being the rear now, relatively secure. There were armed men to guard the station but no active fighting or shelling. The area under the trees was being used to care for men with minor injuries who would be able to return to action. David reported to the first man he saw with a Red Cross helmet and armband. "I cut my head when my boat was destroyed," he said and he removed his helmet.

Another medic spoke to Tim. "Long graze on your shoulder? Let's take you back into the main treatment area."

David's medic had him sit on another hay bale. "That's a lot of blood for a scalp cut," the medic said, examining the helmet and cutting away David's bandage. "More than blood," he said, scraping a little gelatinous material from the inside of the helmet.

"I got the helmet from a dead man," David answered. "I lost my own when I went flying."

The medic was examining the cut. "It's nice and clean. How well can you hold still?"

"Why?"

"We're short on gear. I have what I need to sew your cut but I don't have a place to have you lie down and it's going to hurt like hell when I put in the anesthetic."

"Do I really need stitches?"

"You'd probably get an infection and a bad scar if I leave it open."

David thought a moment. "I can hold still, I think," he said.

For the first time, David noticed a few women, middle-aged, moving among the wounded men. "French mamans," the medic said. "They've been helping us out. Thank God for them."

"Ma mere," David called. "S'il vous plais, aidez-moi."

"You speak French?" the medic asked.

"Fourth Period French. Fourth Period at my high school for three years. We didn't learn much that applies here, though."

One of the women had come over. "You look a lot like my own mother," David thought. "God forbid Mom should ever be in a fix like this." He summoned his French. "Le medecin fixerez mon blessure," he said, haltingly, as he thought through the phrase. "Peut-etre, vous…tennerez mon tete pour lui."

"Hold head for heem," the woman said. "I know little English." She smiled at his attempt, though.

The medic was laying out a few pieces of equipment on the hay bale where David was sitting. He used some antiseptic to mop – paint, really – the area of David's cut. He drew some clear liquid into a syringe. "Novocain," he said. David closed his eyes. The French woman, standing behind him, took his head against her bosom in a vice-like grip. David closed his eyes and put his hands under his thighs.

"Wow, he was right!" David stifled a yelp as the needle probed the edges of his wound. "I've hardly felt that cut, but now fixing it hurts worse than when it happened!" In a few moments the cut was a few inches of burning on his head. The medic asked, "Can you feel this?"

"No," David answered.

"You're ready, then. You shouldn't feel anything in the cut but you may feel some pulling." David did feel some odd pulling sensations. "It feels weird but at least it doesn't hurt," he thought.

"All set," the medic said after what had seemed an hour but was obviously only a few minutes. The French woman released David's head and the medic applied a new bandage.

"You'll have a small scar in the end, I bet," the medic said. "Your hair will cover it just fine. If we'd left it, you'd probably have had a big bald spot." He wrote a brief note. "Have I got your name, your serial number and your unit correct, sailor?" he asked.

"Yes, but what's the big deal?"

"You've just been put in for a Purple Heart," the medic said.

"For a scratch?" David said, incredulous. "You must be joking."

The medic shook his head. "For one thing, sailor, you were only an inch from that Purple Heart being mailed to your family. For another, Purple Hearts will count for something when we win this thing and people start going home."

The French woman was still holding David around his chest. To his surprise, she kissed his bandaged forehead. "Pour tu mere," she said. "Mon fils premier est tombe. My first son...dead, 1940." David hugged her a moment and she moved toward other injured men.

"When did you eat last?" the medic asked.

"We stopped around noon," David answered.

"It's about four in the afternoon now. We're not setting up tables or anything but we'll be passing out rations around six. Will you be all right until then?"

"Yes. But is there someplace I can just sit for a while?"

"Under those trees will do. You can consider yourself attached to headquarters company until we figure out what to do with you. For now you're a working patient. I'll stand as your medical excuse for a few hours at least."

David went over the area where the medic directed him. It was relatively quiet. The day was overcast and cool now that he was trying to rest instead of moving constantly. "I've heard of 'too tired to sleep' but I thought it was just a phrase. And I've got quite a headache suddenly." He found a fairly soft spot under a tree, leaned back, and was out as if someone had turned a switch.

An hour later David woke very abruptly. He was cold and stiff. David saw an outhouse and used it briefly. "It's getting loud here," he thought. Many more people were moving around the aid station. "Hey, sailor," a soldier called to him. "You ready to pitch in?"

"Of course," David answered. He went over to where jeeps were standing, loaded with supplies.

"Join the party, then," the soldier said. David was quickly caught up in a flurry of work. They moved tables and medical equipment into the barn, set up a couple of generators and ran some electrical wires. There were endless buckets of water to be carried from a pump. Many more wounded men were lying on stretchers and bales of hay. And…

"Maman! Ou est maman?" a piping voice, a pitiful voice, was saying. David went to a hay bale and found a small boy, probably about six. The remains of his left leg were bandaged heavily.

"Je ne connais pas tu maman," David thought out in his head and then spoke to the child. "Nous aiderons toi," he stammered out. "We'll help you."

"Je dois pisser," the boy said. He was squirming a little and pointing at his crotch. "I don't remember learning 'pisser' but I can figure this out," David said to himself. He glanced around and saw some buckets. "The little boy needs to tinkle," he said to one of the medics. "Can I use this?"

"That's what we're doing."

David brought one of the buckets over. "J'aiderais toi," he stammered. He could not have the child stand, not with one foot just amputated or blown off. Gently he turned the boy to a sitting position. He lowered the boy's underpants. From the child's confused actions, David realized he was frightened. "Nous somme tu amis," he stammered. "Friends." "I'll have to aim for him," David said to himself. He took the child's penis gently between his thumb and forefinger and held the bucket close with his other hand. The boy caught on after a moment.

A little of the urine landed on the floor and a few drops fell on David's fingers as he put the boy's underpants back in place and helped him lie down again.

David was about to take the bucket outside to the outhouse when he saw several others among the wounded who were squirming. "God, this too is Your service," he said and grimaced a moment.

He went to each of the men in turn. "Do you need to take a leak? I've got a bucket here. Let me help you out." The men's needs for help were sometime very simple, just to hold the bucket and provide a shoulder for balance. But some of the men had bandaged hands or arms and some could not stand at all. Another man saw what David was doing and joined him. "We'll get it done between us," he said. Taking the tasks in turn, they helped men to stand or turn, opened or lowered clothing, sometimes held penises if the injured men could not.

"This is one corner of Hell," David said to himself as they moved from one man to the next. "I don't remember reading about this or seeing it in war movies," he muttered. The stranger who was working with him laughed a moment.

"You hear about the suffering of the wounded and the moans and the fevers," the stranger said. "But somehow Stephen Crane and the biographies of Clara Barton left out this part. Wounded men still have to urinate.

"Walt Whitman knew about it. He nursed in Army hospitals in the Civil War. But even he couldn't put this part into poems."

They were headed to the pump now to wash the bucket after they had emptied it into the outhouse. David finally managed to say, "I don't know what to do if someone has to...doot."

"Move his bowels? Yeah, that's going to be another whole story. This place smells bad enough with sweat and blood and antiseptic and all. You and me, we are doing one of the humblest things that has to be done."

"And the last shall be first," David said. "You know the story of Jesus washing the disciples' feet."

"Of course I do."

"We talked about it in Sunday School once, when I was in high school. Our teacher told us that the disciples' feet would have seemed incredibly dirty to us: wearing sandals, walking in dust, but also mud and urine and dung from the animals in the streets. If Jesus could wash the disciples' feet, we'll find a way to deal with...doot."

"You're kind of shy with your language," the stranger said as they washed their hands in a bucket of relatively clean water and shook them dry.

"I joined the Coast Guard in August of '42. Men have been using profanity around me every day since then, sometimes to my very face. I rarely heard my father or any of my uncles use hard language, though. Got my knuckles rapped the couple of times I tried it, then I realized I hated it anyway and so I never let the habit get me."

"Let's look around that barn some more," the strange soldier said. They went into the dimly lit area near the morgue. There was a workbench and some odd pieces of lumber. There was also an old armless wooden chair. "I was hoping to find something like this," the stranger said. "See how its seat is just a little higher than those buckets we're using."

"Yes," David said.

"Hold the chair for me," the stranger said. He got a bit and brace from the workbench and drilled several holes in the wooden seat so they formed an oval.

"Yes, here's a keyhole saw," the stranger said. He connected the pattern of holes and there was a hole in the seat of the chair. "Let's make sure it'll take weight," the stranger said. David sat on the impromptu commode. "I hope we don't give anyone splinters," he grinned at his friend.

"Are you familiar with files?" his friend asked.

"Reasonably. I've picked up a lot of tool work in the Coast Guard even if I'm hardly a carpenter."

"I've been a carpenter sometimes," the soldier said. "Here's a file that's fine enough for our work. If you'll spend a few minutes smoothing the edge of our commode, it'll be a lot easier on the men's asses."

David filed the edge of the cut they had made and ran his fingers along the rim. "I hope that will do," he said. "What about toilet paper?"

The stranger who had become his friend, though he did not know the man's name, smiled. "We'll have to get along without it," he said. "I was working a supply dump in Sicily when we got hit by a mortar round. It destroyed a crate that contained the only thing we couldn't fabricate and for which there is no real substitute – four miles of toilet paper." Someone called out and the strange soldier looked over. "That's my platoon sergeant. I think we're moving out." He took David's shoulders in his hands and leaned close. "God is with you, sailor."

"And God be with you, soldier," David said. They held hands rather than shaking hands and the stranger went back for his rifle. He was gone a moment later.

David carried the commode chair and a bucket over to the tables that were being used as a work station. "We came up with something," he said and showed the commode to the medic in charge. "Do you want me to make rounds with this?"

"Oh, God, yes, I do. Viktor!" he called.

A man in German pants and suspenders but with no tunic came over. He had bandages on his head and left arm. "Viktor speaks English but he's Russian. He's an EPW who will be glad to sit out the rest of the war. Viktor, this is Sailor."

"I am David," he said.

"You two go around with this contraption and see who needs to take a dump." David winced a moment but at least it was no worse than that.

Yes, it was. "Dump?" Viktor asked, managing to get a surprising amount of accent into a single-syllable word.

The medic nodded. "Scheisse, you know."

"Kind of a nasty word but it's all our Russian is going to understand," David thought to himself.

The range of reactions startled David and he almost wanted to laugh. "God, yes," was the most common answer. Most of the men would manage to use the commode on their own but some were too injured to manage.

"Legs are busted up. Gonna have to have help," and they would take the wounded soldier's arms across their shoulders as he used whatever leg action he could. Most of the men had their hands in good enough condition to manage their clothing.

"My hands are torn up. I've just got my fingertips," a soldier said. He was wearing only his boxers and undershirt. His chest and arms were heavily bandaged.

"Okay," David said. He and Viktor lowered the soldier's skivvies and helped him sit. The man giggled as they put his skivvies back in place and made him as comfortable as they could.

A small man on the next stretcher had one hand off at the wrist and the other entirely wrapped. He nodded and grimaced when David and Viktor came to him. "I gotta," he said.

"I can almost feel how disgusted this poor guy is," David thought. He made sure to avert his face and keep silent. "I bet you hate being helped any time, but this is really hard for you."

David had appropriated a towel and they gave the seat a cursory wipe after each use. Half an hour later, they were rinsing their hands after washing the equipment. "Vell, was very bad," Viktor said.

"Yes. It had to be done." David looked at his hands and then made a show of checking Viktor's hands. "We're clean enough," he said and shook the prisoner's hand.

There were canned rations available now. "Eat first," the chief medic said after looking at David. "You're about worn out yourself. How is your head?"

"I'm not all that hungry," David answered. "My head is stinging but that's all."

"I bet you're dry as a bone, too," the medic said. "Sit down, sailor, and that's an order." He got David a canteen, a can of pork and beans and some crackers.

David began eating by rote, then realized he really was hungry. He ate and drank and felt quite a lot better suddenly.

"Okay. How do you like Viktor?"

"He's all right."

"I'm going to make him your partner for a while. You two work on helping the men who can eat. Some of them can help each other, too, so get them to do it if they can.

"You're also Viktor's guard. I am sure he'll stay put but try to tackle him if he does break."

For the next hour or so, David and Viktor carried the limited rations and water around the barn. The stench was harsh; near the morgue area, it was overwhelming.

David reported back to the admin clerk. "How are things shaping to get back down to the beach? I've got to get back to the Chase."

"I've had word that we should be able to evacuate wounded to the beach in the morning. Sounds like the beach itself is secure, the beach and a small strip in this area. I dunno if the Germans think they can take this area back and I would love to get the patients out of here before they try anything. We'll have you help take the cases we're going to evacuate down to the beach, probably at first light. I'm sure the Navy will get you back to the Chase."

"Obviously, I'm here for the night. What do you want me to do?"

The medic looked at him closely. "For one thing, I want you to sleep some if you can. We've got an exterior guard in case a German patrol gets ideas and we're going to need to keep an eye on the patients all night. Someone told me you speak French."

David made a diminishing gesture. "I speak at French, anyway. I was able to speak to the boy over there."

"I'm going to have you settle down the best you can near him. If you hear him or anyone else who needs help, see what you can do. In between, sleep the best you can. You think you just got a cut on your head but you could have gotten a concussion too.

"I'd like to say you've done your part for one day, but that's not how it works, is it? You're more use here than you'd be at the beach right now and I'm glad to have you."

David looked around the barn; there were probably forty wounded men as well as the French boy. He looked toward the back; there were at least twenty mounds under covers there. "Done my part?" he asked and waved at the shapes.

"Done what you can, at least," the medic answered.

David went over to the young boy's cot. "Petit frere, ca va?" he asked. The boy looked up at him. "Beaucoup de douleur," the boy said. He was crying softly. A medic came over when David raised his hand. "The boy's in a lot of pain," David said.

The medic looked at the notes on the boy's cot. "He can have a little morphine," the medic said. He got a syringe and drew a small amount of medicine into it. "Can you explain?" he asked.

"Pour douleur, pour dormirais," David said to the child, who nodded. The medic wiped a little alcohol on the boy's thigh; the child winced as the medic gave the injection.

"We'll try to get him back to the French tomorrow, as soon as we can anyway," the medic said. "He's the only civilian we're taking care of."

The boy became drowsy a few minutes later. David found a tarp and improvised a pillow on the barn's floor beside the boy. He fell into an achy, dreary sleep himself.

"Hey, sailor, let's go." The chief medic nudged him. "Jeeps outside."

"Yes, sergeant." David pulled himself up and hustled outside. Two jeeps were in the farm yard with litters. David helped carry the first one in and put it on the stanchions. The man lying on it was wearing a German uniform.

"Sailor, search him. Do a good job." The man was speaking harshly in German and his expression was angry, arrogant, hostile. "Cut what's left of his uniform off as you go," a medic said and passed David a pair of heavy shears.

The soldier's tunic was already torn open in front. David cut the sleeves of the soldier's tunic away. He was wearing a long-sleeved undershirt. There was a throwing knife inside the left sleeve of the tunic.

"Yeah, thought maybe so. See his collar?" There were lightning-bolt insignias on the collar. "Waffen SS or somebody like that. Elite, like our Rangers. Dangerous."

"I guess he figures escape is his duty."

"Probably. He'd likely feel good about killing someone on his way out. Keep cutting and keep searching."

"How do I pray for this man, God? His face…" The man's arrogance was obvious even in his wounded and captive condition. "I have to remember that he'll hurt me, hurt any of us. Please, God, help him stay calm. Help him believe we are only going to help him, not hurt him. Help him believe his war is done, dear God. Help me love him even though I'm afraid of him." A doctor and a medic were probing the man's chest injuries, getting ready to put in a tube to drain blood and air from his chest. Someone had already started plasma in the German's right arm.

David moved to the foot of the bed and took the German's left boot off. "Hm. Another throwing knife in a sheath."

"Feel under his sock too," the medic said. David did. "Just his foot."

David pulled the German's right boot off. "Yes, there it is," he said. A small pistol had fallen out of a pouch in the top of the boot.

"Looks like a .25 of some kind. Do you want it for a souvenir?"

"No. I'm sure there's a round in the chamber."

An MP was standing behind David. "I'll take it," he said. "Is there a clearing barrel?"

"Yes, that side of the barn," the chief medic said. "Check that foot too, sailor."

"I think that's all he's got," David said a moment later. "I don't speak German but he might speak French.

"Eh, soldat, plus des armes?"

"Merde. I speak English. More than your French. No more."

The doctor and the medic were ready with their chest tube. David took the German's hands in his own and helped to prop him up.

"Well, you're stoic enough," David said. He watched the man flinch slightly as the doctor used some Novocain to numb an area and then punch the chest tube in. There was a hiss of air and then the medic set up some equipment.

"We've got an area for the German prisoners over there," the medic said. "Got an armed MP to watch them. Let me give him some morphine for pain. I hope it'll knock him out too." David and another soldier carried the German's litter to the prisoner area. A grim-looking MP was standing near with his carbine at port arms.

David went back to the receiving area. Another soldier lay on a litter but the doctor had turned away. "Can you two get this man to the morgue?" the medic asked. "Go ahead and use the litter. Then rinse it and bring it back. The jeep's waiting to head back to the line."

"God, gather this man to you," David prayed as they carried their load to the morgue area. Someone had laid out more blankets.

"Take him by the shoulders and I'll get the legs," the other soldier said. They laid the dead stranger on one of the blankets and folded it over him. More equipment had come up from the beach and there was a pump and hose. They rinsed the worst of the blood off of the canvas. "Dang, that splash is cold," David thought.

There was a lull in the activity. David checked on the French boy; he was sleeping calmly enough. David lay near Viktor and dozed a while. "Huh?" he said as a noise penetrated the fog of fatigue. "Viktor, let's make rounds with the bucket." They went through the tent looking for men who needed to relieve themselves and cleaned up. David dozed again.

"First light, still pretty iffy light," David thought. "I ache in places I'm just finding out I have. My neck especially. Well, a floor and a post are hardly mattress and pillow."

The clerk had a sheet of paper. "Ryerson, my orders are to send you with the first patients this morning. The Chase is already back in England. We'll put you aboard the first transport and they'll be sailing for England when they've got as many wounded as they can handle.

"Let's get these two onto the jeep," the clerk said. David and Viktor lifted the first stretcher onto the mounts on the hood of the jeep and then the second onto the back. "I need you two to hang onto the litters," the driver said. "It ain't much of a road down the draw." Viktor held the handles on the rear stretcher and David took the handles on the front stretcher.

"Movin' out," the driver said. He let in the clutch and started the little truck moving slowly along the dirt road away from the farm.

"Long way," Viktor said. David nodded. The jeep was pretty steady so far. They walked about half a mile before they started down the draw.

"Pretty lumpy," David thought. "Hard to keep footing. Hey, hang on!" The wounded man on his stretcher was sliding against his straps. "How can I get you comfortable?" he asked the man.

"Get me off this damn stretcher and into a real bed."

David chuckled wryly. "Okay, but how about right now?"

"Push my hips back into the middle, will ya?"

"Driver! Can I walk in front of the jeep and hold him that way?"

"Let's keep you on the side. If you go in front, you're too likely to wind up under it."

"Stop a minute, please." The driver did. "Viktor, let's do some rigging. Yeah, wrap the blanket around instead of over our guys. Rig it so you can hold the blanket like a big sling."

"Doing this from the side is kind of complicated," David said to himself. "I've got to stay here, though. If I ride in the jeep, he'll bounce too much, might fall off."

"Viktor, how are you doing back there?"

"Is okay." Viktor was also using the blanket as a kind of sling to keep his patient in the middle of the stretcher.

"Well, this is easy enough," David thought. "The footing's loose and a little steep but okay. The shingle: flat, or nearly. We're sinking into the sand now." A beachmaster marshaled them over to a Papa boat with a number of stretchers already in the deck. "Let's get our men off the jeep." A few minutes later they had their stretchers secured.

"You're the last of this run," the bowman said. They retracted a few minutes later. David jumped up and helped the bowman dog the ramp. "Is this your trade?" the coastie asked.

"Yes, I was coxswain on Lucky 13 from the Chase."

"Chase is back in England already. It may take a couple of days to get you back aboard."

Half an hour later they were alongside LST 388. They were hoisted up and carried their wounded into her well deck.

"How badly are you two hurt?" a corpsman asked.

"Scratched, really," David answered. "Viktor a little worse off than me."

"Would you help us with the men, please? They'll need a drink, a smoke, to take a leak."

"Sure. What gear have you got for us? For one thing, I don't smoke." David fished in his pocket. "One of the few things that survived when I lost my boat," he said.

"My lighter." He flicked it and the flame came up. "I must write Zippo a letter."
"Losing Dad's knife was a lot worse than losing this would have been," he said to himself.

"Why do you carry a lighter if you don't smoke?" the corpsman asked.

"Because a lot of the wounded men smoke."

"Well, here's a pack of cigarettes. Try to go easy on them. I'll give you more when you run out. And here are some urinals."

David smiled wryly. "God has some kind of message for me. I was captain of the head at boot. I was captain of the head at New River – Camp Lejeune, it is now. I was captain of the head on the Chase. I spent last night seeing who needed to...tinkle. And here I am again."

The corpsman laughed. "We probably watched the same war movies. Somehow this never came up."

An hour later the LST, at capacity with wounded, got under. It turned toward the north and they were on their way to England. "It'll take five or six hours, I imagine," David said.

"If we went straight. We have to zig-zag and follow a mine-swept route, so it'll be more like twelve hours," the corpsman told him. "Here's the real head. We'll make sure you get some chow, too."

"Good to have you back, Ryerson. The division is going to need you."

"Mr. Haroldson, I've been asking around for three days now. Do you know what became of my crew? I was with Michael Garret, Phillip Johnson and George Tiller."

The lieutenant consulted a list. "Johnson is hospitalized ashore. Garret and Tiller are fine. We'll get you a new crew member."

"I'm glad they're all right. Or will be. There was a wounded soldier on the boat but I'm sure you don't have word on him."

"No, Ryerson. A lot of men are missing in action. He may have made his way ashore.

"We were lucky. Several boats were destroyed but all of the men came through all right. You know Tyner?"

"Sure, he's the only Negro coxswain I know about," David answered.

"He almost got scalped. There's a big hole in his helmet. I bet he'll show that to his grandkids someday. I see you got banged up yourself."

David touched the bandage on his head. "It's more like a shaving cut, sir," he said.

The lieutenant smiled. "I bet you didn't even shave when you enlisted, Ryerson."

"Only twice a week, sir."

"You've grown up a lot since then. I've seen some of it."

"I've grown up a lot since Tuesday morning, sir."

"We all have. Or at least we've aged.

"I've read your after-action report. I put you in for a Bronze Star."

"How many of us have said, 'Thanks, but I was just doing my job?' Or 'Thanks, but I was just trying to stay alive?'"

"So far, all six of you."

"Ryerson! Got three for you. The usual from Millford – lucky you. This one's intra-theater."

David took his letters to his bunk. "Mom and Andrea, of course. Third Battalion, First Infantry Division? Major Iblings? Bulky." He opened the envelope and found both a typed letter and something sandwiched in cardboard.

"Dear Bosun Ryerson

"I'm sure you remember meeting me but I think we missed introductions. I'm the captain who organized the patrol you were with on D-Day. I made major a month or so later. I've been too busy to write until now – it's been a long walk from Normandy to Paris and west from there.

"I've lost touch with Corporal Moore and Sergeant Greene but they were safe when I last heard of them.

"I am enclosing a memento of our day together at Omaha Beach. This is the Combat Infantry Badge, awarded for thirty days of combat service. Your uniform regulations won't permit you to wear it on your blouse, I know. I wanted to send it as a token of the respect you earned on D-Day. I hope you will remain safe yourself and that all of us will be home for Christmas.

"Best Wishes,

"Kevin Iblings, Major, USA, Infantry."

He opened the cardboard fold. A silver badge, a rifle in a wreath, lay in his hand.

"Dear Major Iblings

"I received your kind letter today. I'm glad Tim and the sarge were doing well – I pray they still are. All of our friends will remain in jeopardy until we end this horror. God's will be done in this and all things.

"Thank you for the badge. It will have a place of honor in my home and in my life. I pray God will bring you and all the men in your charge through safely. I fear it will not happen – you and your men will almost certainly suffer losses. I pray God will gather all of your lost men – they will never be lost souls.

"With my thanks again,

"David Ryerson, BM2C, USCG"

David laid the badge in his locker next to a small case. "I got the Bronze Star in official mail, too," he thought. "So many heroes there isn't time to honor each of them. That takes a Navy Cross, like Lieutenant Gill at Salerno. I kind of stick at calling myself a hero – God gave me fortitude when I needed it. God gives me fortitude when I need it.

"I have a feeling the dreams are going to be part of my life forever."

"Long Way to Go"

"It's just a three-day pass, Mom. I've had more chances to get home than a lot of the men so I said I'd spend the holidays aboard."

"Then we'll have Thanksgiving a week early," Mom said. "Dad will meet your train. He'll have help."

David hung up and paid the thirty-cent tab for the call. "Help. Andrea, of course. I wonder what chats Mom and Andrea have had since February. Andrea and her parents."

"Yes, there they are," David thought as the train stopped. He got off with his suitcase and hugged Andrea, kissed her quickly. He hugged Dad and they shook hands.

"You two sit in back and I'll make like a chauffeur," Dad said. David held Andrea's hand and she leaned into him as they drove to the house. "Dinner at Andrea's tonight, full-dress Thanksgiving tomorrow," Dad said. "I don't know how we'll get over Mom's feast tomorrow in time for regular Thanksgiving."

Andrea's parents were welcoming as always. Her dad drew David into the parlor as he was about to help with the dishes. "You're doing enough KP," he said.

"I'm a second-class now, Mr. Matthews. I'm finally off captain of the head and KP. I have to assign those jobs now."

"Glad to hear it, but sit with me anyway." David took the rocker near Mr. Matthews' wing chair.

"This is just a little like an audience with the skipper," David thought.

"There's a lot on my mind, David. I wanted to speak with you in private. Not secret – by all means talk with Andrea about what I want to talk about. But I wanted to talk man-to-man."

"Still writing myself man," David said as Andrea brought them coffee and vanished again.

"Andrea knows what I want to talk about anyway," Mr. Matthews said. "Are you two in love?"

"Yes, Mr. Matthews."

"But you're not engaged."

"No, sir. We're not even going steady. Too much going on. I have to take into account that I may be flitting in and out for another couple of years. The Germans are on the ropes but they're still swinging – 'home for Christmas' looked good in September but we were too hopeful. And the Japanese are terrible fighters. That looks like taking two or three years yet."

"It's terrible, son. And you're right. The end looks as far now as when you enlisted."

"Closer than that – we can see what the end looks like, at least. But we're going to have to invade Japan. Every Higgins boat in the Navy will be on that - - and every coastie driving them.

"And not every coastie is coming back from those landings, Mr. Matthews. I get past that with Andrea as fast as I can. We both know it. That's the biggest reason we've been holding back on promises."

"But you're being faithful to Andrea when you're away."

David laughed. "Faithful to Andrea, yes. Maybe also faithful to an idea that Andrea stands for. The men who meet girls and have flings – I understand that. Lonely, very little pleasure in our lives. But I'm not lonely. I have my family and I have Andrea and I even have you and Mrs. Matthews. I have people to come home to."

"Especially Andrea."

"Yes, sir. Especially Andrea. But I won't take a promise or offer one. I'm a lot more man and Andrea a lot more woman than a year ago. But we're still very young. When the war is over, I have to put a new life together. If we make promises after the war, it may be a few years yet before we can bring them to life."

"That's a very manly take, David. Very mature."

"It's also frustrating. I know it is for me and Andrea says the same."

"It's a cost of the war, I'm afraid. And I'll tell you this: you may not have taken a promise from Andrea, but she's made one to herself. I think you've made the same one."

"What do you hear from Walter and Steve? Andrea said they are both safe so far."

"Walter's in Southern France and Steve is somewhere in Belgium. They've both seen action but, yes, they're safe so far. That's about all they can tell me. They write about camp life and barracks life a little; the campaign in Southern France was easy at first but now they're working their way into the Alps and closer to Germany, so I bet it's getting tougher for them."

"David. I heard something and wondered if it was you. It's three in the morning."

David had a cup of tea in front of him. "Thanks for checking, Mom. My sleep is weird from watches on the ship. And I've had weird dreams since Sicily."

"Nightmares, David?"

"Well, yes. Nightmares. They've been worse since June."

"Your father has them once in a while. He says almost everyone who's been in combat has some touch of shell-shock. It eats some of them alive."

"We talked about it a little bit. Well, it never ate Dad alive. With God's love, it won't get me either. But it sure changed me."

"Ryerson! Yes, two from Millford. Somebody likes you, Ryerson."

"What news, then? Oh, no. God in Heaven, no."

"We got the telegram just last night. There's almost nothing left of the German Army and they should have quit fighting weeks ago...but Walter was in the wrong place at the wrong time and he was killed. Walter was killed...I can barely write the words."

"Dear God, gather Walter to you. Be with his family now. Be with my family, too – Walter's death will make them more afraid for me."

"The Japs have surrendered! The Japs have surrendered!" Word flashed through the ship a lot faster than the official announcement did.

"We hit them with some kind of new bomb. Took out two whole cities. They finally believe they're licked."

David thought that over. "Two entire cities. And I've heard about what we've been doing to other cities, especially Tokyo. Dear God, gather all those souls, please. And help all of us who are living to put a stop to this.

"When do we start going home?"

That question was also on everyone's lips. There were pockets of resistance on scattered islands. There was an empire to occupy and manage. Two months later, though, the word starting coming in.

"You sent for me, bosun?" David said as he entered the warrant bosun's office.

"Yes, Ryerson. Early last year, we had a conversation about OCS and you asked me to take you out of consideration. This time, I'd like to know if you're thinking about making the Coast Guard a career now that the war is over."

David shook his head. "I've been considering the advantages, bosun. Crowded quarters, small pay, months away from home. A bed that bounces around like a roller coaster if there's any sea on. I'll admit the food's been pretty good.

"I'm sure you know my answer sir. It's been three eventful years but home is calling me much louder than the sea."

The bosun laughed and nodded. "I was quite sure. Then I have important news, news you'll want to get into your next letter. Even tonight."

David's heart rose. "Here it comes. I've been doing the arithmetic."

"Yes, you have all your points. When we reach San Diego with this first load of Army and Marines, you'll be the first one discharged. This is your trip home. We sail tomorrow. Meantime, of course, you're still in the deck department, still responsible for your boat."

"The boats will just be passengers on this trip," David said.

"That's right. They'll have an easy trip and you'll work as hard as ever. Congratulations. I've still got a few years until I plan to retire, but it's time for your life to get back on course. Dismissed, son."

David wrote two letters that night. They began much the same. "I'm hoping this will reach you before I get to San Diego. I'll be home for Christmas – and I'll be a civilian.

"To the family, now.

"I can probably enroll in college for the spring term. I'll finally be a freshman! I've picked up a lot of practical engineering and now I'll start the formal training. There are plans to help us all find jobs and attend college if we want to. I doubt I'll enroll full-time, though. I'm used to working eighty hours a week, so I plan to work and attend school both."

"To Andrea. Oh, to Andrea. My biggest bet until now was five pieces of candy on an acey-deucey game. And now I'm going to bet everything I hope for. But I have to hold just a little back."

"Sweetheart, you know how often I've thought about you. The only day you were off my mind was June 6 of last year – the day we landed in France. I hope you'll understand but I was busy. And I had a headache.

"We've kept a little distance these three years now. No promises that we'd regret, no ties that might become chains. No lost husband or fiancé if I was killed. Or worse, just vanished as so many have.

"And that's been the right thing to do until now. But now...please think of what's next."

"Congratulations, Mr. Ryerson. And I must say, you've taken good care of your pay. That's one of the larger mustering-out checks I've issued."

David returned to the barracks and took off his uniform. He folded it carefully. Another "casual" looked at him.

"Feels like putting yourself back on, eh? Just a couple of days for me," the young stranger said. He watched as David donned a white shirt and a tie, a double-breasted suit, a pair of oxfords. He came and took David's hands, both of them, in his. "We've been on a long journey," the stranger said. "And now you go to start a new path, a new life. So will I. Dominus vobiscum, pal."

"Et cum spiritu tuo," David answered. "So you've been a roaming Catholic?"

"I'm a Methodist," the stranger smiled. "I just like Latin. Studied it in high school – four others and me. Let me take your seabag so you can manage that foot locker."

They got David's gear into the bus. At the train station, David sent a telegram: "Home around 9pm Sunday. Please tell Andrea." He tried to tip a redcap who took his gear. "No, sir, I watch for you boys. I know you by your hair, by your walk. You're on your way home. You boys going home now, you been in the longest. Thank you, son."

"The United States is about three thousand miles from coast to coast. It's a three-day run to Philadelphia and another hour home. Hour by hour, home. Mom. Dad. Dan. Marianne. Diablo is gone – I'll miss the old cuss.

"Andrea. What does she think of my last letter? What do I think of it? I'm sure she knows what I have in mind but I want to do the job right. This isn't a request through channels for furlough."

The miles rolled. "Returning soldier? Coast Guard? Join us, will you? What'll you take?"

"That's very kind of you. Just a coke, please. Promised my mother, you know."

"Where have you been?"

"Just now? Brought home a load of Army men -- Christmas presents for their families. Mustered out in San Diego. As far from home as they could get me."

"See much action?"

"Some."

"You look like you just mustered out, young man."

"Yes, sir. Coast Guard finally sending me home."

"The sailor's money is no good in this dining car, porter. Get him a good breakfast – ham and eggs. My wife and I will pay the tab and gladly. I'm Bill Tilden and this is Nancy. Our daughter, Christina." She was a bright teen, chatty and pleasant, as were her parents. He found himself visiting with them through the morning.

"Have you been gone long, David?" Bill asked.

"Depends on which yardstick you're using. I was home for a few days about a year ago, but I went into the Coast Guard in summer of '42."

"Seen much?"

David smiled. "I've been in Europe and then the Pacific. We went through the Canal, so I didn't get all the way around the world. I was a coxswain on a Higgins boat – the small one, we called it a Papa boat. My last trip was to bring home men from the Pacific."

"How were they?" Bill asked seriously.

"Some were recovering from wounds. Some were okay. Some of them had looks...you know what the Pacific fighting was like. From what the men told me, even worse than in Europe."

"We can imagine. We read about it and we saw some newsreels. Only the men who were there know, though."

"I was too young for the Great War, had a deferred job for this war."

"Sir, you and the people at home won this war, you know. You built what we needed, you grew our food, you moved more stuff than anyone's ever moved before. The factory people who made the M-1 saved my life. We could only be the battle front because you were the home front."

The family detrained in Chicago; both the mother and Christina insisted on kissing him. "Have to get you ready for your mother," the woman said.

"And your girl," Christina added with a twinkle in her eye. "Andrea, I think you said."

Through the Alleghenies – "Charleston! Charleston, West Virginia!"

"It's starting to feel real," David thought. "It's hard to believe. I've been dozing and reading for three days and things are a little fuzzy."

He went to the small lavatory with his clean white shirt. "I've washed up with less than this," he thought as he shaved and sponged himself. "This is as spruced-up as I can get."

The redcap in Philadelphia took his quarter and said, "Welcome home, soldier."

"Coast Guard," David smiled.

"You're all heroes. Welcome home."

"A long hour," he thought as the train passed through the dark landscape. Then it was slowing. Then it was stopped.

Then he was on the platform. Andrea was first to hug him, to take a kiss on her lips. Then Mom and Marianne. Then Dan and Dad were shaking his hand, pounding his back. All the people in the station applauded. "Welcome home! Welcome home!" he heard.

"I was tired until the train stopped. Now I'm as awake as if I were taking on a landing party," David thought.

"You sit in back with Andrea and the kids," his parents said. He held Andrea's hand and scarcely said a word as they drove to the house; Marianne on his lap and Dan were taking up all the slack. They had a snack in the kitchen and David finally got enough space to say, "It's time I walked Andrea home."

They were seated on the porch swing, wrapped up against the clear, cold night. "You've been fumbling in your pocket since we left your house," Andrea said.

"So I have. I was going to explain a lot about the next couple of years. I have a plan. I hope God will bless my plan. But explanations will wait.

"I bought a few civilian clothes in San Diego. And this."

David knelt and Andrea's eyes grew large and bright. He opened the small box. He took the ring out and placed it on her extended hand. "It needs to be sized, looks like."

Andrea pulled him to his feet, pulled him against her, and they kissed with open mouths for the first time. "Thank You, God, thank You," David breathed. "Thank You, dear Jesus," Andrea echoed.

The front door burst open. Andrea's parents hugged them both. "The David Ryerson that came home is finally showing some sense about women," her mother said. "Finally."